THE MONSTER IN THE LAKE

LOUIE STOWELL

illustrated by
DAVIDE ORTU

Walker Books

Text copyright © 2019 by Louie Stowell
Illustrations copyright © 2019 by Davide Ortu

First US edition 2022
First published by Nosy Crow (UK) 2019

Library of Congress Catalog Card Number 2021943994
ISBN 978-1-5362-1494-9 (hardcover)
ISBN 978-1-5362-2230-2 (paperback)

21 22 23 24 25 26 LBM 10 9 8 7 6 5 4 3 2 1

Printed in Melrose Park, IL, USA

This book was typeset in Chaparral Pro.
The illustrations were created digitally.

Walker Books US
a division of
Candlewick Press
99 Dover Street
Somerville, Massachusetts 02144

www.walkerbooksus.com

To my parents
LS

To my friend Stella
DO

This new notebook belongs to Josh. Hands off if you are not Josh. If you ARE Josh, please read on.

If you are Alita or Kit, you can read over my shoulder if you like but no adding anything.

And if you are Kit, no getting dirt on this book. It's new!

Dear Future Josh,

You will probably have many exciting things happen to you in the future, where you live, so here are a few notes to help you remember the exciting things that have already happened.

By the way, are you running the country yet? Did you stop global warming? Are you a famous writer? I can't wait to get to the future to find out!

Here's what's happened recently. At the beginning of the summer, our friend Kit discovered that she's a wizard—the youngest one in the world as far as I know, and I know a lot. Alita and I discovered that we aren't wizards yet (boo), but we did help to save the world (yay). Here are some other important facts you need to know about wizards and our summer so far . . .

1. Wizards are real, but they don't all have long white beards or pointy hats. They DO have cloaks, though, and our local wizard, Faith Braithwaite, wears a lot of dangly star earrings and very bright lipstick.

2. Every wizard has a second job: running a library. This is because underneath every library sleeps a dragon. If that dragon wakes up, terrible things happen. So when a librarian tells you to shush in a library, it's to save the world from fire and chaos, not because they're trying to spoil your fun.

3. At the start of the summer, an evil businessman named Hadrian Salt tried to wake the dragon under our library because he

wanted to use its power to become
a wizard. Kit, Alita, Faith, and I
stopped him, using magic, books, and
our brains. My brain in particular.

4. Some books in our library are
magical, and I'm not allowed
to read them out loud unless
Faith is there. Book spells are
so powerful that the spells can
start working even if you're not
a wizard. There are other magical
books, too, called portal books.
You can use them to travel huge
distances between libraries.

Portal books are also really fun
because it's like you're inside the
book. For example, there's one
that's a book about gardening and
you get to walk through all these
beautiful gardens. The ones with

dangerous animals and monsters
in them aren't as fun, though.

5. Beneath the library is a forest
that we like to call the Book Wood.
It's also known as the stacks, and
it's where all the really magical
books are kept. Over time, some
of those books turned back into
trees, and their pages turned into
trunks and leaves, covered in spells.
I am DEFINITELY not allowed to
read the spells on the book trees.
They're some of the most powerful
spells in existence, and apparently
I might blow myself up. Kit's not
allowed to read them yet, either.

6. I think that's it. Oh, wait, no.
I haven't said anything about the
dragon who sleeps under our library!
She's called Draca, and it's part of

our job to read to her—it helps
her stay asleep and makes sure
her dreams are full of stories.

7. Me and Alita have been helping
Kit train to become a wizard.
Faith is teaching her because Kit
is too young to go to the Wizard
Academy. Kit's getting better at
magic, but she still makes a lot
of mistakes. She also doesn't like
reading, so it's up to me and Alita
to learn all about how magic works
so we can tell her when she's wrong.

Josh out!

PS: Josh forgot to add that there's a half
dragon, half dog named Dogon who lives in the
library. Dogon is the sweetest little creature
that ever lived. He breathes the cutest fire.
Also, it's mostly Josh who's always telling Kit
she's wrong.

Alita xxx

I TOLD YOU NO ADDING ANYTHING, ALITA! AND I DON'T ALWAYS TELL KIT SHE'S WRONG— ONLY WHEN SHE IS WRONG!

PPS Come on, guys, you've been riting in this notebook for practically HOURS. Let's go and do something fun. This is summer, not skool!

Kit

KIT, THIS IS MY BOOK. STOP WRITING IN IT! YOU DON'T EVEN LIKE WRITING! YOU DIDN'T EVEN SPELL "WRITING" RIGHT! AND WE CAN GO OUTSIDE WHEN I AM DONE.

OK. I AM DONE.

Josh out again, with this notebook going in a SAFE place this time.

CHAPTER 1
MISS-SPELLINGS

In the Book Wood beneath the library, Kit Spencer was practicing spells. She was a stocky girl, with red hair, pale skin, and more mud than you'd usually see on a person who wasn't a professional pig wrestler.

At that moment, Kit was wearing her (not-yet-muddy) wizard's cloak and hovering a ball of fire above her head. Her tongue was out, and her face was screwed up in concentration. The goal was to raise the fireball above her head, then lower it to the ground. So far, so good . . .

Faith was guiding her through the spell. The

librarian was a tall, dark-skinned Black woman with expressive eyebrows. She was wearing a long, fluorescent-yellow dress and a chunky blue necklace. Her hair was in long locs, and her elegant nails were painted the same electric blue as her necklace. Unlike Kit, she wasn't wearing a cloak; mostly wizards only wore those for ceremonies and parties. But as a wizard in training, Kit wore hers to track her progress. Each time she learned a new spell, her cloak gained an extra stripe of yellow at the bottom. She currently had a band of yellow about the width of her hand.

She was hoping that at any moment she'd be getting her Controlled Fireball spell stripe. She was so close!

Faith stood beside Kit, watching the fireball intently. "Now, slowly . . . use the gesture I showed you . . . and slowly, *slowly* lift the ball a few inches. That's it. Gently . . ."

Kit was concentrating so hard that her forehead was a wall of sweat. This was the hardest spell she'd tried so far. The words of the spell weren't hard: just a quick "*Feuer, oben*" at the beginning. But after that, you had to focus your mind so hard that it felt like you were going to burst a blood vessel somewhere deep in your skull. Kit could feel the magic flowing through her as she focused on the fire, keeping it in its ball shape, keeping it steady . . .

She lifted her hands just a little. The fireball wobbled and dipped.

But then it rose, slowly, slowly . . .

Kit felt something new building inside her. She'd never managed to get this spell to work properly. Was this what it was supposed to feel like? It was intense! Almost painful . . .

"I'm doing it!" Kit cried. "I can feel it worki—"

At which point the fireball flew up into the air and exploded like a firework over the treetops, scattering light of every color.

"AAAAAARGH!" Kit shrieked, shaking her hands as if they were on fire, then tripping on a root and tumbling backward onto her bottom with a bone-jarring *BUMP*.

"Are you OK?" Faith rushed forward to help her up, checking her over for injuries. "You're not burned, are you? Or in any way broken?"

"No, I . . . don't think so." Kit's bottom was bruised, but the heat of the spell had all flown upward. She peered above the trees to where the fireball had exploded.

"Where did it go?" she asked.

Faith waved a hand. "There are protection spells over the trees, to stop any rogue magic from damaging the library. They absorbed your fireball spell." She smiled. "So don't worry; it's safe to make mistakes down here."

Kit screwed up her brow. "The thing is, I thought the spell was working. I mean . . . it *was* working. I just don't know what went wrong. Something felt . . . weird." She looked down at her cloak. No new yellow stripe. Her heart sank.

"Well," said Faith, "it's a bright sunny day out there—maybe you got distracted? I'm guessing you actually want to be outside. Maybe you need a break?"

Kit felt annoyed. Sure, yes, she *did* have a habit of getting distracted. And yes, it was a sunny August afternoon, and every other child her age was outside in the park or at the swimming pool. But she *hadn't* gotten distracted. Not this time.

Faith picked up the pile of books they'd been using and ushered her toward the exit of the Book

Wood. "Come on. I think that's enough work for today. Break time."

"I *didn't* just get distracted, though," said Kit, not wanting Faith to think she was lazy. "I felt something. Just before it went wrong, I had this . . . this rush, here." She put her hand to her chest.

Faith gave her a curious look. "That doesn't sound right," she said. With the books balanced in the crook of one arm, she pulled something out of her pocket. It looked like a tiny silver flute but had a little blue gemstone at one end instead of a mouthpiece. She pressed some little keys and the gemstone glowed red.

"What's that?" asked Kit.

"Thaumometer," said Faith. She held it away from her and waved it around, back and forth, in front of Kit. "It measures magic. Hmm . . . The wild magic readings in the air are a bit high, even for down here near the dragon." She shook the thaumometer and looked at it again. Its gemstones were lit up like a Christmas tree, and it emitted a faint hum. "Perhaps it picked up the extra magic in my pocket.

Too many magical objects in there; I need to do a clear-out." She patted a large pocket in her dress, which lay flat against her hip and didn't appear to have anything in it. But it rattled as she slapped it. Faith's pockets were like that: infinitely full of stuff, but always looking empty. Kit had begged to learn the spell that made them like that, but Faith had told her it wasn't a specific spell—just what happens over time if you stuff enough magical items into a normal pocket.

"Now, you go out into the sun and have fun. I have a meeting at the Wizards' Council." She pulled some sunglasses out of the flat pocket. "Can't forget these."

The Wizards' Council was in charge of magic throughout the country, and all librarians had to attend meetings with them at least once a year.

The members of the council were very old and very grumpy, and their meetings were so long and dull that Faith admitted she sometimes took a nap halfway through.

"The trick is to wear sunglasses," Faith had said. "They don't know you're asleep if they can't see your eyes."

Kit escaped into the sunshine, glad for once that she was only a trainee wizard.

CHAPTER 2

THE PARK

Once out in the warm, fresh air, Kit went to find her friends Alita and Josh. As she expected, they were lying underneath a tree, reading. Alita was curled up around her pile of books like a neatly dressed dragon guarding a papery hoard. Her black hair was, as always, perfectly braided, and her skin had the healthy brown glow of someone who always ate their fruit and vegetables without having to be bribed. In fact, she had a little container full of mango that her mom had packed her. Kit wasn't sure how it was physically possible, but Alita managed to eat the mango while reading without getting yellowy-orange stains all over her pale-blue dress.

Tall, skinny Josh had tight dark curls, brown skin, and an expression of extreme concentration. He was taking notes as he read. Josh never went anywhere without a notebook. He had an amazing memory, but insisted he needed to write everything down "for posterity." Kit wasn't sure, but she thought posterity had something to do with your bottom.

Josh was reading a book on Arthurian legends and wizard history, which Faith had found for him in the stacks. He'd put a blanket on the ground to lie on, partly to keep himself from getting grass stains, but also to protect the book.

Alita had her own blanket and had spread out several books. She had the latest Danny Fandango— *Danny Fandango and the Crown of Bones*, which she'd just read for the fourth time that summer—and now she'd moved on to another, even fatter book, *The Lord of the Rings*. Kit thought a book that long would give you a permanent wrist injury. Trying to read it over Alita's shoulder certainly made Kit's brain feel injured.

"Hi, Kit!" said Josh. "Did you know King Arthur was actually a wizard, and Merlin wasn't?"

Kit told him she had not known that. She wasn't a hundred percent sure she needed to, either.

"So," Josh went on, full of excitement about his new discoveries, "Merlin was a fake who tried to steal Arthur's power! And Guinevere was a wizard, too, only her story got covered up by history because back then people thought only men should be wizards."

"History sounds annoying," said Kit. "What are you reading, Alita?"

"I'm just up to the part where Frodo arrives in Rivendell with the other hobbits and Strider," said Alita, as if Kit should know anything about those people or places, or what a hobbit was.

"What's wrong?" asked Alita, seeing Kit's gloomy expression.

"My spell blew up," said Kit. "Big fireball, boom." She threw herself on the ground next to them, gaining some new grass stains on her knees, shorts, and T-shirt in the process. "And now Faith probably thinks I'm lazy."

"What went wrong with the spell?" asked Alita.

"Did you get the hand gestures right?" asked Josh. He demonstrated the correct way of performing the gesture to lift the fireball.

"Yes!" said Kit. "I swear I did."

"Even the part where you lock your elbow?" asked Josh.

Alita nudged him. "Kit knows what she's doing, Captain Cleverclogs," she said.

"I do! I did it right!" said Kit, with a grateful look at Alita. "But it was like the magic was misbehaving."

"Are you sure you didn't pronounce the words wrong?" asked Josh, giving her a skeptical look.

Kit rolled her eyes. "Fine, don't believe me. Let's go for a walk." She picked up her friends' books. "Wow, these are heavy."

"Not if you're sitting down reading them," said Josh hopefully.

But Kit stared until Josh and Alita reluctantly picked up their blankets and left their reading spot, strolling down toward the lake to look at the ducks.

A dog walker was coming toward them. Kit thought it looked like the best job in the world, just walking around the park with a pack of dogs. There was a German shepherd, a dachshund carrying a stick in its mouth, a tiny Chihuahua, a big pit bull with the sweetest face that Kit had ever seen, and, all in all, more dogs than Kit could count. Alita was grinning even more widely than Kit.

"So. Many. Dogs," she whispered.

A large dog broke away and squatted to pee, and the pack came to a halt. The dog walker gave the children a toothy smile. "Would you like to say hello?" He gestured to the dogs. "They're all very friendly."

Alita didn't need to be asked twice. Cute dogs needed petting. She got down on her knees, carefully laid down her enormous book on her folded blanket, and started stroking a fat little spaniel, scruffling its ears. Kit crouched and started patting the dachshund. It was very wriggly and a little cranky-looking. Being a walking hot dog was apparently a very difficult life.

Josh was less delighted than the girls. "What if they lick me?" he asked distrustfully.

"That's the point!" said Alita. "Awww, this one's licking my face!"

"That's not hygienic," muttered Josh.

As the two girls were on their knees, petting several dogs each and giggling as the dogs tried to lick them, Kit heard a voice. It was like no other voice she'd ever heard. It was snuffly and eager and excited. She couldn't tell where it had come from, but it definitely wasn't human, she knew that much.

"Mmmm. Goose poop!" it said.

CHAPTER 3

THE VOICES

Kit looked at Josh and Alita. They were looking around, trying to figure out where the voice had come from, too. Josh knelt beside the girls.

"What's happening?" he whispered. "Did you both hear that?"

Kit and Alita nodded.

The voice spoke again. "Poop! I found goose poop! It's mine now! Going to roll in it! Mmmmm! It's so goosey!"

As the voice spoke, the German shepherd rolled onto its back and rocked back and forth on the grass with a look of delight on its furry face. "Stop that!" said the dog walker. "Bad boy!"

Another, higher-pitched voice said, "There's a stick. That's my stick! I want that stick!"

"Kit, I think *they're* talking," whispered Alita. She pointed to the tiny Chihuahua, which was now chewing at the dachshund's stick on the ground.

"Fascinating!" said Josh.

"How is this happening?" asked Kit.

"It has to be magic!" said Alita, gazing around at the talking dogs in wonder.

Meanwhile, the spaniel seemed to be getting annoyed that Alita had stopped stroking it and put its paw on her knee, licking at her hand.

"More! Human! Friend!" it said. "Give me more pats!"

Alita blinked. "Sorry," she said, and continued patting the dog. "They're not just talking. They're talking to *us*!"

The dog walker chuckled. "They do seem like they can talk sometimes," he said.

"I don't think he can hear them talking," Josh said under his breath. He smiled at the dog walker. "Cute dogs."

"Thanks!" said the dog walker.

"Thanks," said an intelligent-looking collie.

Kit knelt to stroke it. "Who's a good boy?" she asked, feeling a bit awkward.

"I'm a girl," said the collie. "But I am good. I'm a good girl."

"Why are you talking?" Kit whispered, stroking the collie and leaning close so the dog walker couldn't hear her.

"I'm always talking," said the collie. "It's just that usually no one listens. Can I have some bacon?"

"Excuse me?" said Kit.

"Bacon. Since I have your attention. I'd really like some bacon.

I'm always telling people I want bacon, but they never listen. Bacon?"

"Sorry. No bacon," said Kit, feeling sad about disappointing the incredible talking dog.

"I'd better get going," said the dog walker. "I have to keep up the pace or they all start deciding to wander off in different directions! Have a nice afternoon!"

"Bye!" said the collie. "Bacon next time?"

The children watched as the dogs trotted away, chatting as they went.

"Poop again!"

"Bacon!"

"SQUIRREL!"

The children stared after the dogs for a moment.

"What just happened?" asked Kit.

"A spell?" suggested Josh. "You didn't do that, did you, Kit?"

"I haven't learned a spell that makes animals talk," said Kit. "I would definitely remember learning that! I'd do it every day!"

"Another wizard, then?" suggested Alita. She

looked around them. The park was busy. There were people everywhere—having afternoon picnics, playing Frisbee, and walking their dogs. "How do you spot a wizard?"

"Well, according to the book Faith gave me, there are no obvious signs, unless you have special equipment, like a thaumometer," said Josh. "Wizards look just like you and me. Or Kit, obviously."

"Let's walk around—see if we can spot anyone doing spells," said Kit.

They couldn't see anyone who looked like they were doing magic. No one waving their hands suspiciously, or muttering words in the mishmash of languages that made up magical spells. Not a single obvious wizard anywhere.

But as they passed a flock of crows all clustering around a tree, they heard something.

"Get off my perch, you bunch of scraggly pigeon-lickers!"

"It's my perch, not yours!" said a second crow. "Get your own perch, you tatty-feathered slow-flapper!"

"Hey, crows!" Alita called up to the tree. "Can you understand us?"

The children heard some whispering, and then a bird flew down and landed on the ground, blinking up at them with its black eyes.

"We understand you. But we don't know why," said the crow.

The bird peered up at Kit.

"Wizard," it said. "I smell wizard. Did you do this?"

"No, I swear," said Kit.

"Humph," said the crow. "It's usually wizards. Don't trust wizards. Oh! Worm! Crowkind, alert! Worms!"

The rest of the crows flocked down and started pecking at the ground, ignoring the children and feasting on delicious, wriggly worms.

Kit, Josh, and Alita moved on. As they reached a wooded part of the park, they heard some squeaking voices. It took a while to figure out where the voices were coming from, until Alita knelt and pointed. "Ants!" she said. "There's a colony living here."

But although the ants were saying words in English, none of it made any sense. Each ant on the ground would squeak out words, seemingly at random.

"Earth!"

"Magic!"

"A!"

"Change!"

"New!"

"Coming!"

"Beneath!"

"Hungry!"

"Wait," said Alita. "Insects are hive creatures. They do everything as a group. So each ant isn't going to say anything interesting. We need to put it all together. Maybe the order of the words doesn't matter?"

"But I don't think we can hear *all* the ants speaking," objected Josh. "They're spread over too wide an area. So we'd probably miss some words."

"We could go around recording them all," Alita said, "then put it together afterward?"

"Or we could just try to find a creature that makes sense on its own," suggested Kit. She'd spotted a water vole in the undergrowth by the lake. "Hey!" she called, waving at the vole.

It gave her a distrustful stare.

"No! Not talking to you," said the vole. "Humans own cats. And dogs. Dogs eat voles. Humans are bad news!"

"I promise I won't hurt you!" called Kit. "And I don't have a dog!"

"But I have food," said Alita, trying a different approach. She pulled out a bag of chips from her skirt pocket. The vole looked interested.

"I'm listening . . ." It scuttled closer.

Alita held out her palm with some chips in it.

Kit wondered if putting your fingers within biting range of a toothy little mammal was a good
idea, but the vole came up quickly and nabbed the
chips from Alita's palm, then scuttled back to a
safe distance.

"Why can you talk?" asked Josh as the vole
nibbled.

"Why can YOU talk?" asked the vole. "You can't
normally. Just human noises."

"Have you noticed any-
thing weird?" asked Kit.
"Like . . . anyone doing
magic spells?"

"Don't know about
magic," said the vole.
"But there's something"—
it glanced around conspira-
torially—"something
new here. More
chips?"

Alita shook her
head.

"Bye!" said the vole, and it disappeared into the undergrowth again.

"The animals in this park are VERY unhelpful," said Josh grumpily.

"I think they're just hungry," said Alita. "I'm not very talkative when I'm hungry."

"It's too bad there aren't any monkeys here. I bet they'd be better at explaining things," said Kit. "'Cause they're more like us."

"Crows are actually very intelligent," said Alita. "But I don't think they care much about us and what we want. I wouldn't, if I were them. They're interested in crow things."

"If the animals aren't going to be helpful, how are we going to figure out what's going on?" asked Josh.

"Well, no one else seems to be able to hear the animals talking," said Kit. She gestured to the other people in sight. Everything else seemed normal, and no one was running around screaming, "OMG! Talking animals!"

"Maybe it's because we're kids," suggested Josh.

"Adults are too closed-minded to see stuff they don't expect to see? That's how it is sometimes in Danny Fandango."

"But there are other kids here, too," said Alita. She pointed to a small boy not far away, playing fetch with a spaniel. There was no sign that they were having a conversation.

"So it's just us who can talk to the animals," said Kit. "That would make sense if it were just me because I'm a wizard, but you two can as well, so . . ." She frowned. "How can we find out what's going on?"

Josh and Alita both smiled at once. Kit didn't like those smiles. "I know," said Josh. "We can go to the library and RESEARCH!"

"Or . . . I could do a spell?" suggested Kit.

"Or we could research."

"So . . . we're going to go and sit inside and read books on a day like this?" asked Kit.

"Exactly," said Alita. "Yay! Books!"

"Yay," said Kit, in the least "yay" voice imaginable.

CHAPTER 4

THE LIBRARY

When they arrived at the library, they asked Greg, the assistant librarian, for help. But when they described what was happening, Greg shrugged, making his long white beard sway. "Talking dogs? Not my problem," he mumbled. "Plus, I'm taking off in an hour. It's almost five and I don't want to be starting anything complicated that'll make me late getting home. Golf is on."

At the best of times Greg was not very helpful. And when Faith was away, he was even less helpful, because being in charge of the library alone put him in a foul mood.

"Please, Greg," said Alita. "Are there any books about this sort of thing? Has it happened before?"

Greg grunted. "Nothing new under the sun. Everything's happened before, one time or another. Try the magical history section in the stacks."

So the children headed down to the library stacks, through a bookshelf at the back of the library floor. Kit pulled at one of the books and said the spell that opened the door.

"*Labba!*"

Her fingers glowed, and the entire shelf slid silently aside.

"That never gets less cool," said Josh.

Kit grinned. He wasn't wrong.

"Let's go," she said. "*Ina,*" she added, touching her forehead and focusing on the air above her. A magical light appeared, and they walked down the dark, book-lined corridor that led to the Book Wood. The books themselves sat on shelves, but today Kit and her friends were interested in the corridor, which was where the magical history books were kept.

They ended up with more books than they could

carry, so Kit had to perform a lifting spell to take some of the weight, which she couldn't manage at the same time as the light spell, so they stumbled out of the corridor in darkness, scuffling and bumping until they emerged into the light of the spell-book trees.

"I love magic and everything, but next time," said Josh, "I'm going to bring a flashlight."

In the Book Wood, the smell of old paper mingled with a fresh, green smell. Kit smiled. It always gave her a little bubble of joy when she walked down there. A forest beneath a library, where the trees were alive and magic filled the air.

"Where's Dogon?" asked Alita.

Usually, the little half dog, half dragon would rush to see Alita, his favorite human, whenever she came down there, but today he was nowhere to be seen.

"Maybe he's sleeping," said Josh.

"Well, he is half dragon," said Alita. "And they sleep all the time, so that would make sense. But I wish I knew where he was."

They sat in the common room, which was inside

a huge tree in the middle of the forest. Josh had a book on his lap and was reading out passages.

"Apparently animals have started talking without anyone performing spells at different times throughout history. Usually when something big was going on in the magical world."

"Like what?" asked Kit.

"Like . . . during a war between wizards," said Josh. "Or when a dragon was waking up."

"Oh!" Alita sat up very straight. Her eyes were wide. "You don't think it could be because Salt nearly woke our dragon?"

Josh thought about this. "Well . . . maybe. That was a month ago, though, and in this book it said all the weird talking-animal stuff happened at the same time as the dragon waking up."

"Maybe a dragon is waking up now, and it's just happening somewhere farther away," said Kit. "Should we tell Greg?"

"He didn't seem worried that animals were talking, though," said Alita. "Surely he'd know if a dragon was waking up."

"I suppose so," said Kit, not feeling entirely comforted. Greg never quite seemed to be in the same world as everyone else, so she wasn't sure whether his being calm was a sign that everything was fine. Kit suspected that Greg's beard could be on fire and it would take him ten minutes to notice.

"Didn't Faith say the Wizards' Council was being extra cautious at the moment, keeping an eye on all the dragons to make sure none of them were at risk of being woken up?" said Alita. "After what happened with Draca and Salt?"

"Maybe we should ask Draca herself what's going on. Whether she's feeling wakeful . . . or another dragon is," suggested Kit. "I mean, surely dragons know more about dragons than books do!"

"But I've still got ten books I haven't even looked at yet!" Josh complained.

"Well, why don't I go talk to Draca while you keep reading?" said Kit.

"Hmph!" said Josh, who was already deep in the next book. "Good."

"I'll come with you, Kit," said Alita. "I want to ask Draca where Dogon is. It's not like him to hide."

Kit and Alita descended the stairs to the dragon's cave beneath the Book Wood. Kit felt her stomach tighten as she reached the bottom of the staircase. What if the dragon *was* waking up again? The building wasn't shaking, at least. That was a good sign. When Salt had nearly woken Draca, the whole building shook, and smoke rose up through the library.

Sure enough, when Kit entered Draca's cave, the dragon was fast asleep. Little puffs of smoke rose out of the nostrils of her long snout, drifting up to the high stone ceilings. Kit held out her hand to Alita. "Should we join her dreams?"

Alita took her hand and grinned. "I could spend days in there," she said. "You know, if it wouldn't drain you of all your power and leave you as limp as a wet sock."

They'd have to be quick. It took a lot of magic to remain in the dragon's dream, especially if you were taking someone who wasn't a wizard in there.

The two girls knelt beside the dragon, and Kit put one hand on Draca's flank, holding Alita's hand with the other. The dragon was cold to the touch, and her scales were rough with sharp edges. Kit's fingers began to tingle as the dragon's magic flowed through them.

"Tickles!" murmured Alita, feeling it, too.

A rush of heat washed through Kit, then everything went dark.

When the light returned, they were inside the dragon's dream. Today, Draca was dreaming of a stone road leading to a castle.

The dragon was sitting in a field of flowers beside the road, watching them curiously with bright-green eyes.

"Friends!" said Draca. "Welcome!" She gestured around with her claws. "Someone read this book in the world above last week. Or years ago. Or now." She shook her head. "Human time is hard for me."

Kit smiled. She'd been the one to read the book

in the library for storytime last week. It was set in a magical land with a wizard and a fight against evil.

"I'm glad you liked it," said Kit.

"You feed my dreams," said Draca approvingly.

"It's a good story," said Alita. "Though it's not as good as the Danny Fandango books."

Draca's eyes lit up. "Will you read me the new one soon? *Danny Fandango and the Crown of Bones*?" she asked. As the dragon spoke, their surroundings changed. Now they were in a stone room with cross-shaped windows. Draca was curled up on a vast, dragon-sized four-poster bed, and the children were sitting at the foot of it.

"Where are we?" asked Kit.

"Lara Fandango's bedroom from book two, in the High Tower, when she and Danny are adopted by a queen! Only her bed isn't usually that big," said Alita.

"It's my dream," said Draca. "Everything is me-sized here."

Draca grinned, showing her shining fangs. No matter how often Kit came to see Draca, she could never quite get used to chatting as friends with a creature that looked like she could eat you in a single chomp.

"I would never eat you, Kit Spencer," said Draca.

Alita laughed. "Don't think bad thoughts around mind-reading dragons, Kit."

"Sorry," said Kit, blushing. "I forgot."

But Kit's mind wasn't the only one that Draca could read.

The creature turned her scaly head toward Alita. "You are worried about Dogon, aren't you? I'm worried, too. The little one has been visiting me in dreams," said Draca.

"You mean, like we are now?" said Alita. "I didn't know he could do that."

"No, when he sleeps, he wanders into my dreams. He's been wandering more lately."

"You mean, he's been sleeping a lot?" Kit asked.

"Yes," said Draca. "He came to play with me when I was on a ship sailing around the world, and when I was with a monkey who set fire to a city full of demons."

"I hope he's not sick," said Alita.

"But he is," said Draca. "And he's getting weaker. I'm sorry."

"Oh, no!" said Alita. She gripped Kit's hand, and Kit gave hers a squeeze back.

"We came to ask something else, too," said Kit. "We wanted to see whether you were feeling like waking up? Or if you know of anything else funny going on with magic?"

Draca didn't reply at first. Her eyes fixed on the distance, and a little burst of flame rose out of each nostril with a huff, as though she were sighing. Around them, the world shifted. Sparkles of magic filled the air, moving gently at first, then beginning to whirl faster and faster, until Kit felt dizzy.

"There's . . . something new," said Draca, above the whirl of magic. "It's not above, not in the library. It's beyond. Where things are green and there is water . . ." She shuddered. "Something is not quite right. Something sad."

"What does that mean?" asked Kit.

"Green . . ." said Alita. She tapped Kit's arm excitedly. "The park! It's something in the park!"

"Someone is there. Someone new. Too much wild. Too strong."

The whirling magic faded around them and was replaced with an image of the dragon's cave. Draca let out a little roar.

"Are we bothering you?" asked Alita, looking worriedly at Draca. "You're not . . . waking up, are you? If you are going to wake up, please tell me so I can warn my family to get out of town!"

"Waking up? Hmm . . . I'm not sure. I think you should go upstairs and read me a story, just in case," said Draca with a sly grin.

Alita grinned back. "Sneaky Draca. But I love you anyway."

"I do think we need to go," said Kit. "I feel . . . drained." She yawned. Her body was heavy, and her mind felt like sludge.

To leave the dragon's dream, all Kit had to do was say goodbye.

"Bye, Draca! See you soon!" she said, and with a flash of black, they were back beside the sleeping dragon.

Kit felt utterly exhausted, like she'd just run a mile in lead shoes, carrying her entire family on her back.

"Phew!" she said. "I'm not looking forward to the stairs."

"Want to sit for a bit?" asked Alita.

There was a little stone bench outside the dragon's cave, and the two girls sat. The stone was cold against Kit's bare legs.

"What do you think that meant, about the park?" asked Kit.

"She said there's someone new," said Alita. "A wizard, maybe? Visiting from somewhere?"

"Maybe. But Draca said 'too much wild,' and wizards don't bring wild magic with them. That comes from dragons," said Kit. "And I think Draca would've mentioned another dragon, if there were one living under the park."

Alita thought about this. "Yes, wild magic comes from dragons . . . but not *just* dragons. Other magical creatures give off wild magic, too."

"They *do*?" asked Kit.

"You should read more," said Alita.

Kit groaned. "I don't think I could physically read any more than I do already. I think I have librarian's elbow from turning too many pages."

"That is absolutely not a thing," said Alita.

After a rest and a very slow climb, they rejoined Josh upstairs in the common room.

"I've found something!" he said, tapping his book and looking up in excitement.

"Us, too! Draca was really helpful!" said Alita. "Though she also said Dogon is sick, which is . . ." She trailed off, biting her lip. "But what did you find?"

"I read that too much wild magic in a single place can cause spontaneous spells, such as—check this out—animals talking! But also . . ." Josh was pointing to places in his book, then flipping pages faster than a human could possibly read. Or at least faster than Kit could. "Too much wild magic in a place can also make wizards' spells go wrong!"

Kit almost yelled with relief. "I *knew* I wasn't getting that fireball spell wrong! It was wild magic, not me!" She started doing a little victory dance. Then she stopped when she realized how sore and tired she was from keeping Alita and herself in Draca's dream. She sat down on a chair ever so gently.

"What did Draca tell you about what's making the animals talk?" asked Josh.

Alita told Josh their theory that there was a magical creature living in the park that shouldn't be there. Not a dragon. Something else.

"Could it be underground?" asked Josh.

"It could be living in a sewer beneath the park," suggested Alita. "Maybe it's a magical rat?"

"That's gross," said Kit. She grinned. "I LOVE IT!"

"I hope it's not a sewer creature, though," said Josh. "My mom would kill me if I came home smelling like sewage."

"Speaking of coming home, my mom's expecting me for dinner soon," said Alita.

"Should we go and search the park tomorrow, then?" asked Kit.

The others agreed. "Just wait a few minutes, though," said Alita. "I need to go look for Dogon.

Draca said he's sick, and he's been sleeping a lot, and I know all his favorite places for naps."

Alita came back a few minutes later, holding Dogon in her arms. The furry, puppy-like creature was still half-asleep, letting out little drowsy growls. She put him down, and he stretched out his red wings and took a few feeble steps.

"Are you OK, Dogon?" She turned to the others. "I found him sleeping beneath a tree. He'd made a nest out of moss."

"Rrrrrrr!" Dogon growled. As though to prove he was fine, he flapped groggily into the air, displaying his scaly green belly. He only made it a little way before he started to sink to the ground, exhausted.

"He's really not himself," said Alita. She knelt to stroke Dogon.

Kit and Josh clustered around.

"His scales look sort of . . . flaky," said Josh.

"Maybe it's not serious?" said Kit. "Maybe it's just . . . like a magical cold?"

"I don't like it," said Alita. "I wish the wild magic were making Dogon talk. Then he could tell us what's wrong." Alita put her hand on Dogon's head, and he leaned into it, demanding pats.

"When Faith comes back, maybe she can take him to a dragon vet?" suggested Kit.

"When *is* Faith coming back?" asked Josh.

"She didn't say. Just that she had a Wizards' Council meeting," said Kit.

Alita carried a sleepy Dogon to a soft patch of moss and laid him down to rest. She looked back at him, frowning. "Should we leave him alone while he's sick?" she asked.

"I'm sure he'll be OK," said Kit, trying to sound certain.

CHAPTER 5
WILD MAGIC MAKES THINGS WONKY

arly the next morning, they met up by the tennis courts to search every inch of the park for magical creatures. Kit got briefly excited when she spotted a flash of dark fur in the bushes by the bathrooms, but when she followed the creature into the undergrowth, it just turned out to be a large German shepherd. It looked at her, panting.

"There was a vole!" it said excitedly. "I think it's still here!"

"You haven't seen . . . some kind of magical creature, have you?" asked Kit.

"Don't know about magical creatures. But there was a vole!" said the dog. "A big one. I'm going to eat it! Or make it my friend. I haven't decided. VOLE!" It put its nose to the ground and snuffled off through the bushes.

"Anything?" asked Alita, following Kit. Josh was behind her, peering around for any rogue monsters that might come leaping out of the bushes.

Kit shook her head. "Just a dog. It was talking, but it was just a dog."

"That means that whatever the creature is, it's still around somewhere," said Josh. "If it weren't, the talking spell would have worn off by now, wouldn't it?"

"I don't know where it could be, though," said Kit. "Maybe it *is* time to try the sewers? How do you get into sewers, anyway? Maybe one of those metal covers on the ground? Oh, I know! I learned a spell to reveal hidden entrances." She lifted one hand and lowered the other toward the ground, thinking about the sewers beneath her feet. "*Pradarshan!*" she said.

A wobbly glowing light appeared, beaming from the tips of her fingers and pointing toward a metal grate in the ground near the edge of the lake.

"There!" said Kit in delight. The spell had worked! Nothing had gone wrong! "That's the way into the sewers!"

"Wait," said Alita. "Maybe we don't need to go into the sewers quite yet."

"Oh, good!" said Josh.

Alita pointed to a bush, not far away, at the edge of the lake. "Notice anything weird?"

They went closer, and Kit saw that the bush had some leaves missing. It looked as though something had taken a bite out of it.

"It wasn't like that a few minutes ago when we came past," said Alita. "I think whatever it is . . . is near."

The children instinctively huddled closer together, glancing around.

"I wish Faith were here," said Josh. "She'd know what to do."

"Wish granted," said a voice.

They turned, and there was Faith standing right behind them. She was holding her arms aloft, and her dark eyes sparkled like gems.

"Wait," said Josh. "Do you . . . do wizards . . . grant wishes?"

Faith laughed loudly. "HA! No, they just know how to make an entrance." She lowered her arms, and her eyes stopped sparkling. "I spotted you three across the park coming out of those bushes. I've been here a couple of minutes. I thought I'd just wait until you noticed me. You really need to work on your observation skills."

Kit went red. "I was distracted. We're looking for a monster."

"And Dogon's sick!" added Alita. "He's gone all flaky and floppy! Draca said he's getting worse, too!"

"A monster? Dogon's ill?" said Faith. She looked serious. "Catch me up."

They filled her in on their hunt for a wild-magic-creating monster in the park, the talking animals, and Dogon's flaky skin and worrying sleeping patterns—plus the fact that they had just found a bush with a bite missing.

"So with all this wild magic flying around, my spell going wrong this morning wasn't my fault." Kit thought it was very important to point that out.

"I see." Faith nodded. "Odd, though. A visiting magical creature could definitely cause animals to talk, and disrupt your spells, but it should settle down in a matter of hours, not last for days." She looked thoughtful. "I'll worry about that in a moment. Go on. What else do you know?"

"Well, we don't know what kind of creature is behind it all, or where it is," added Josh. "But we do know it likes the taste of bushes."

Kit looked at the bush with the bite taken out of it. She looked beyond it. There was another bush with snapped twigs, closer to the water. Something very big had been that way. "I think"—she pointed behind her—"it might be in the lake!"

Faith pulled out her thaumometer and held the object in front of her. Its gems began to glow brighter and brighter. To Kit's surprise, Faith stepped right into the lake. The thaumometer glowed bright red and started to emit a squealing noise like a frightened pig.

"Well. That answers that," Faith said.

CHAPTER 6

THE MONSTER IN THE LAKE

We need to talk to it, whatever it is," said Faith, after doing a quick spell to dry and clean her dress. "But we can't have the whole park listening in. Do you remember the cloaking spell we did last week, Kit?"

Kit tried to think back. "Was that the one that went wrong and I ended up making my face invisible but nothing else, so it looked like I had no face, and Josh almost got sick?"

"I remember," said Josh with a shudder. "That was so wrong. People should have faces."

"It wasn't even *your* face that went missing!" pointed out Kit. "It was worse for me!"

Josh shook his head in disagreement. "If it *had* been my face I wouldn't have minded, because I wouldn't have been *able* to see it, so it wouldn't be as creepy."

Faith cleared her throat. "Do you think you can do the spell correctly this time, Kit? So that you cloak the area around us and prevent anyone else from seeing or hearing anything they shouldn't?"

"Maybe you should do it," Josh suggested to Faith. "Since Kit's magic is going wonky."

Kit glared at Josh. He might have been a genius, but if there were an intelligence test for tact, he'd score negative points.

"She'll be fine," said Faith. "It's not a big spell, and I'm right here to help if she needs it. Kit?"

Kit nodded. She mimed the word and gesture to herself before saying it out loud. In spite of nerves that felt like a bag of fighting cats in her stomach, she took a deep breath and performed the spell. "*Skor!*"

She felt the usual rush that came with any spell, and the sunshine dimmed a little. She looked at Faith, who nodded.

"Good," said Faith. "It worked."

Kit pointed at her face. "All there?"

"All there," said Josh, looking relieved.

"Well done. Now." Faith gestured to the lake. "Let's see who we have here."

"How do we summon . . . whatever it is?" asked Alita.

"I like to use a little spell I call . . . yelling," said Faith. "Hey!" she shouted. "You in the lake! You know who I mean. Whoever's not supposed to be there. Come out! It's safe . . . but we'd like to talk to you!"

There was a moment's silence, and then the water began to ripple outward from the center of the lake, and a dark shape rose to the surface. A smooth little head popped up, about the length and shape of a large dog's snout, but earless, with beady eyes on the sides of its face. It blinked at them.

"How did you know I was here?" it said. It spoke with an accent. It sounded . . . Scottish? Kit wasn't very good at recognizing accents. The creature raised its head a little farther, showing a long neck. It looked around nervously. "We're cloaked, right? I felt the spell . . ."

"Yes, we're perfectly safe," said Faith. "We only found you because you're causing the local wild magic levels to spike." She looked thoughtfully at the creature. Its face was lined with sadness.

The creature bit its lip and looked down into the water. "I'm sorry if I'm causing trouble," it said. "I just don't have anywhere else to go."

"How did you get here?" asked Kit. "Did you come through the sewers?"

The creature made a face. "No. Ew! I came through a water portal. From Scotland."

Kit heard Josh gasp next to her. "Are you . . . the Loch Ness Monster?" he said. "I've read about you!"

"No, I'm not, and no, you haven't!" said the creature, looking displeased. "I'm not fame-seeking! Not like that Nessie." The creature wrinkled its snout. "I'm Lizzie! I'm what's known as a Lesser Nessie by some, though I've always found that insulting. I'm not lesser. I'm just . . . more low-key, you know?"

"Oh," said Faith. "I *have* read about you! There's a book in my friend's library in the Scottish Highlands about the—" Faith hesitated.

"You were going to say Lesser Nessies, weren't you?" said Lizzie.

"Let's say loch creatures of a more subtle style," said Faith.

"Loch creature is right," said Lizzie. "I'm from Loch Lochy."

Kit thought that was a very unimaginative name for a lake. It might as well be called Lochy McLochface.

"So what brought you here?" asked Alita.

"Mermaids," said Lizzie, her mouth turning down and little wrinkles appearing on her slimy forehead. "They kicked me out. Barred me from my own loch. So I came here."

Kit blinked. "Wait, what? Mermaids?" She wasn't so much shocked that mermaids were real, but that they were living in a lake. "I thought mermaids belonged in the ocean."

"Some do, some don't," said Lizzie. "Just like fish. You get freshwater mermaids and saltwater ones. And these particular mermaids . . . well. They were never any trouble until their leader, Morag, got it into her scraggly head to kick me out. She claims the lake is for mermaids only now.

She said I had to leave. I'm not a fighter. I like a quiet life, and she's scary when she's angry. So I left and came here."

"Why here?" asked Kit. "It's a long way."

"The portal was open," said Lizzie. She sniffed. "You can't blame me for coming in. You left the door open."

Faith gave a little sharp breath. "Oh."

Kit looked up at her.

"I'll tell you later," said Faith. "Now, Lizzie, you being here is a problem. It's disrupting the levels of wild magic."

"I could go somewhere else," said Lizzie, looking a bit sad. "Though I was just starting to get comfortable. You've got some tasty bushes around here."

"I'm afraid you going to another lake wouldn't solve the issue," said Faith. "I think I can see the problem. Ordinarily, a magical creature relocating would cause a bit of trouble at first, but only for a few hours, and it certainly wouldn't make other magical creatures sick. But you being kicked out . . ." She shook her head. "Your sadness has thrown your own wild magic out of whack, making it surge. You're affecting all the creatures around you—magical and non-magical."

"And wizards," added Kit. "Well, me, anyway."

"Och, I might as well stay here, then," said Lizzie. She blinked her black little eyes and shrugged her flippers. "I can't win. It'll be just as bad somewhere else, won't it? Because I'll be just as sad."

"You can't stay here, I'm afraid," said Faith. "We've been having some issues with talking dogs."

"And insects. And rodents. And birds," added Josh.

"Is that bad?" asked Kit. "No one else noticed but us. Why *did* no one else notice?" she asked Faith.

"You've spent time around the dragon—you, Alita, and Josh—not to mention read a lot of magical books. And you're a wizard, Kit . . . so"—Faith gestured around her at the park—"you're all able to see things other people can't."

The children exchanged pleased glances.

"We're like those dogs that can smell explosives!" beamed Josh.

When Kit and Alita gave him funny looks, he added, "That sounded cooler in my head."

"Well," said Lizzie, "since only these . . . unusual children can see me, I don't see why I can't just stay here." She sniffed. "A few talking dogs that only you people can hear won't do anyone any harm."

"Not yet," said Faith. "But if you stay much longer here, your magic will affect things more, and eventually we'll have *everyone* noticing magic. And we all remember what happened last time a powerful person found out about magic." Faith gave a pointed look at the children.

"I don't," said Lizzie.

"There was a man named Salt who found out about magic and tried to wake the dragon, and it was bad," explained Josh. "I have the longer version written down in my notes if you'd like to read?"

Lizzie blinked in surprise. Her mouth opened and shut again. "A woken dragon!"

"Semi-woken," corrected Josh.

"We got her to sleep again," added Alita.

"Well, that explains why your water portal was open," said Lizzie.

The children turned to Faith questioningly.

"I'll explain later," said Faith.

Lizzie shook her head. "Well, I don't like to be a bother, but I don't know what to do. I can't go back while the mermaids won't let me . . . and they've started peeing at my end of the loch." Lizzie shuddered. "They've threatened worse if I come back."

"But if you stay, your wild magic will do all kinds of damage," said Faith.

Alita gave a little gasp. "I think it already is. Could that be what's making Dogon sick?"

Faith frowned. "I think you're right."

"Sorry about your dog," said Lizzie. "I can't help you, though. I'm too scared to go back." She began to sink.

"Wait," said Kit. "We can talk to the mermaids for you. Maybe we can get them to change their minds."

"Be my guest," said Lizzie. "But don't get too close. Remember, they pinch . . . and bite. And pee!"

With that, she sank beneath the surface of the lake.

They walked back to the library, all feeling glum. Faith explained all about water portals, and Josh scribbled notes as he walked, which meant he bumped into a lamppost halfway back.

Water portals connect lakes and streams and other bodies of water all over the world, using magic. All water is connected, and you could have a portal from anywhere to anywhere, in theory, but someone has to open them. If they were open all the time, you'd end up with magical creatures in swimming pools or even your bathtub, and that would be freaky.

When Salt nearly woke Draca,
that opened the water portal
here to the one where Lizzie is
from. Faith says it should have
closed naturally in a day or so.

They gathered in the shabby, cozy common room in the Book Wood beneath the library. Alita had Dogon on her lap. He was trembling and had snuggled into her like a baby.

"We can't leave him here," said Alita.

"I'm afraid you're right. He'll only get sicker while Lizzie is here," said Faith. She came over and knelt next to Dogon, giving him a pat. "Her unstable, sad wild magic is really bad for him."

"Oh, no!" said Alita. "Poor Dogon!"

"I think we should take him away from here until we can persuade Lizzie to leave," said Faith.

"Can't we just cheer her up?" suggested Kit.

Faith shook her head. "I'm afraid nothing will cheer her up except returning home. Magical creatures can be very attached to the places they come from. They're not very adaptable. That's what happens when you're millions of years old."

"But if we take Dogon away . . . Won't it be bad if we take him away from the dragon?" asked Alita. "Isn't that the source of his magic?"

"Not if we're not away too long," said Faith. "He's got enough dragon magic in him to keep him healthy and happy for at least a week away from Draca."

"Wait, a *week*?" said Josh, looking alarmed. "Where are we going? What will I tell my mom? I'm supposed to be back in time for dinner at six tonight! That's in eight hours! If I'm away a second longer, my mom will flip! My dad will BACKFLIP!"

"Easy. No one's going away for a week," said Faith. "I'm hoping we can get all this wrapped up long before your families even start worrying about where you are."

"My ma worries even when I'm *with* her," said Alita with a half smile. "But as long as we're back for dinner, she'll keep her worrying to her normal speaking voice, not her shouting voice."

"Where *are* we going?" asked Kit, whose own parents probably wouldn't notice if she were several days late for dinner.

"Well, I was thinking we should go to Scotland to investigate the loch. How does that sound?" asked Faith.

Kit thought it sounded excellent. "I've never been to Scotland!" she said.

"You'll like it. It's very . . . outdoors," said Faith with a smile.

"How will we get there?" asked Alita. "I don't think my parents would let me travel on my own. Even with you, Faith," she added apologetically. "And wouldn't that be expensive?"

"Not if we go by book!" said Faith.

"A portal book?" asked Kit excitedly. These were the special books wizards used to travel between libraries. Each book took you through a different landscape on your way, depending on what the book was about. Some of them were safer to cross than others.

"So what library will we be going to?" asked

Alita, focusing on entirely the wrong part of their journey, as far as Kit was concerned.

"Invergloy," said Faith. "It's near the loch where the mermaids live, Loch Lochy."

"Are there libraries by lochs? Like, in the middle of nowhere?" asked Josh, wide-eyed.

"Sort of," said Faith. "You'll see when we get there."

"Can we take Dogon to Scotland with us?" asked Alita. She hugged the little furry dragon creature tight.

"Yes, definitely," said Faith. "He should start feeling better as soon as he's away from Lizzie." She got up and went to a cupboard underneath the sink. "I think his carrying case should be under here. Usually I'd let him fly, but the poor thing can barely flap right now. Hmm . . ." She pulled out a bottle of some kind of glowing liquid, a pair of high-heeled shoes, a can of paint with a label reading HEX-RESISTANT PIXIE HOUSE PAINT, and a small statue of an octopus with what looked like diamonds for eyes, until she found what she was looking for. "Bring him over here."

Alita carried Dogon over and put him in the carrying case, which was bright red and hovered just above the ground.

"I could use one of those for my school books," said Josh, impressed. "How does it work?"

"A fairly simple levitation spell, kept going by crystals in the base of the case," said Faith. "The crystals act like batteries for magic, you see."

"Cool!" said Josh, scribbling notes in his little book.

Alita gently encouraged Dogon inside the case. He made a grumpy sound but was too tired to resist.

"Right. Let's get him out of here," said Faith. "I'll just call ahead to let the librarian know we're coming. Would you get a portal book? Invergloy has all the same ones as us aside from *Dangerous Animals*."

"Good," said Josh. "That one's terrifying."

Kit went to the shelf where the portal books sat and unlocked it with the spell Faith had taught her. She picked one she hadn't used before, called

Inside a Computer. It was a large book, with bright pictures and flaps to lift.

When Faith came back from calling the Invergloy librarian, they were ready to go. Kit started reading the book.

"Computers are like libraries, but instead of books, they store information using zeros and ones . . ."

They found themselves inside the book. It wasn't like some of the other portal books, where you walked through a realistic landscape. In here, lines of light surrounded them, forming a sort of cage. Beeping sounds filled the air. Kit saw some moving platforms ahead, and old-fashioned robots bustled around looking busy.

"Is this what a computer looks like inside?" asked Alita doubtfully.

"No, this is how Kit imagines it would look," said Faith.

"It looks like a computer game!" said Josh.

"Well, that's what you find inside any good computer," said Kit. "Which way do we go?" she asked Faith.

Faith pointed to the moving platforms. "That way. We'll have to jump a bit. Dogon's case will just float behind us."

They started to make their way through the

book, hopping from platform to platform. It wasn't too hard. In fact, Kit loved it. She made a mental note to use this book as often as possible when they traveled between libraries. It was safer than the *Dangerous Animals* portal book, but a lot more fun than the garden one.

When they got to the end of the moving platforms, they walked through a shining door made from light. The next page of the book was a room with green walls and a green floor, all covered in silver wires.

"It's a circuit board!" said Josh.

The next room was full of ancient computers, covered in dust.

"This is the page about the history of computing," said Faith.

"Oh, I think my nan has that one," said Kit, pointing to a big, box-like computer.

One of the machines didn't even look like a computer—it had a hand crank on one side, and lots of what looked like metal cogs.

"Oh, wow! A difference engine!" said Josh. "It's an early version of a computer! From hundreds of years ago!"

"Sometimes I wonder if there's ANYTHING you don't know," said Kit.

"I don't know the rules of baseball," said Josh after a moment's thought. "I should learn them soon!"

The next room was full of robots. Some were just arms, building and painting a car. Kit could smell the fresh paint. It made her feel giddy. Another was playing soccer with itself.

"This one looks almost human!" said Kit, marveling at a robot with skin that looked surprisingly realistic.

"Thank you," said the robot. It was dressed as a butler and had a mustache. "How may I be of service?"

"Can I have some toast?" asked Kit.

The robot pressed its stomach, and out popped hot buttered toast.

Kit had to be dragged out of that room, clutching two wedges of perfectly browned bread.

"Come on," said Faith. "Remember what happens if you stay in one spot in a portal book?"

Kit did. You risked going into a trance, and if you stayed too long . . . you might not be quite right again once you returned to the real world.

"What happens if you *die* in a portal book?" asked Kit, about to take a bite of her toast.

"It's best to avoid it," said Faith. She pointed at Kit's toast. "And I wouldn't eat that either."

Kit dropped the toast hastily. As it hit the ground, it disappeared in a cloud of square pixels. Kit gulped.

"I bet eating *that* would've given you indigestion," said Josh, watching the toast pixels float away.

After a few more pages, they reached the end of the book—a vast wall of screens, flashing images showing people going about their business, including one group of men who Kit thought were almost definitely robbing a bank.

"Don't worry. It's not real," said Faith. "All part of the book."

Kit could never get over how real portal books felt when you were in them.

"What's the library called again, where we're going?" asked Alita. "This is the end of the book, right?"

"Yes, it's a really short book," said Josh sadly.

"The library's called Invergloy," said Faith.

"Invergloy, hus!" said Kit.

They appeared inside what seemed to be a metal container, about the size of Kit's living room at home. A strip light glared down on them from the ceiling. The walls of the box were lined with books, and there was a window at one end, through which Kit could see . . . seats?

"Oh! We're inside a van," said Kit, making sense of the space at last.

"It's a mobile library," said Faith.

There was a clanging sound, doors opened, and natural light streamed in through the back of the van. The sky outside was gloomy. A man was looking up at Kit suspiciously. "What are you doing in there?"

He had a big black beard and curly black hair, pale white skin, and very arched eyebrows. His clothes were dark and scruffy, and he wore shorts and big walking boots. When he saw Faith, his expression cleared, and he gave a huge, welcoming grin. "Ah! It's you! I didn't know you'd be here so soon."

"Hello, Duncan," said Faith. She held up Dogon's carrying case. "We were in a hurry. We had to get this little one clear of . . . Well, I'll tell you all that later."

"Who're the bairns?" He peered into the van.

"I'm Kit," said Kit. "This is Josh and Alita. Thanks for letting us come through your . . . library."

"Sure. Well, come on out! Hot day like this, you'll be baking in that van." Duncan gestured out at the rolling moorland behind him.

"It's not hot," said Josh. He peered out of the van at the gray sky. He shivered ever so slightly in his T-shirt.

"Around here, this is beach weather," said Duncan. He held out his hand and helped the children down. "Welcome to Invergloy Mobile Library."

Kit looked around. They were standing on a sloping, wide-open landscape covered in scrubby plants and dotted with rocks. The van was parked on a dirt road. The air smelled fresh.

"Who uses this library?" asked Kit. She couldn't spot anything but grass and little purple plants. "I can't see anyone around."

"I drive around all the local villages so people can

borrow books. Plus, I run a festival every summer. People come from all around to listen to stories. But I was on my way home just now. I only stopped to collect some supplies." He gestured to a pile of freshly picked plants.

"Are they for spells?" asked Josh, looking excited.

"Well, that one is . . . and that one," said Duncan, pointing to a couple of different shrubs. "But that one's for my lunch. Wild rosemary grows around here."

"Sounds delicious," said Faith. "When we've done what we came to do, perhaps you could make us some lunch?" She grinned, looking at Kit and the others. "Duncan's an *excellent* cook."

"And an all-right wizard," added Duncan. He waggled his fingers. "I'm no Faith, but . . ."

Faith didn't contradict him.

"So how can I help you?" asked Duncan. "You mentioned Loch Lochy in your message."

"Message?" Kit had a thought. "Can you get a phone signal out here?"

Duncan shook his head. "Nope. No signal out

here at all. But we wizards don't need phones to send messages, do we?"

"Nope." Faith pulled a small, globe-shaped stone out of her pocket, about the size of a golf ball. It was a milky, swirling color, as if someone had poured white paint into water. It seemed to be glowing from within, giving off pulses of light, as if it were alive.

"Wow! What is it?" asked Kit.

"Wizards call it a duradar. But most people would probably call it a crystal ball," said Faith.

"Can it see the future?" asked Josh.

"Not unless the future is 'you're about to have a cup of tea that you've just asked a wizard friend to put on for you when you arrive,'" said Duncan. "It's basically just a wizard phone."

Josh looked a little disappointed.

"On the plus side, it has *great* reception absolutely everywhere, and you never need to pay a bill," said Faith. She held out the globe for them all to take a look. Kit took it in her hands. It vibrated lightly, making her skin tingle. She wondered if she'd ever get one of her own.

"Can you point us in the direction of the loch, Duncan?" continued Faith. "Maybe give us an introduction to the mermaids?"

"Yes to directions. It's that way." He pointed at the path behind his van. "But I can't introduce you, sorry. I'm nae going near those mermaids again in a hurry. They spat at me last time I went by. And threw a rock at my head!"

"They sound like fun," said Faith, pursing her lips.

"They weren't always like that. They've been very private people, and a bit grumpy, but they were never aggressive before, and they always lived in peace with the other loch creatures. I don't know what's got into them." He shook his head. "But I went fishing down at the loch the other day. I'd asked their permission the week before and they'd been fine, then suddenly . . ." He shrugged. "Well. I won't be going back in a hurry."

Kit thought these mermaids sounded much more interesting than the drippy creatures she'd read about in fairy tales, who seemed to spend their time pining after princes and sitting around on rocks.

"Let's go meet them!" said Kit.

"Agreed," said Faith. "But I think we should leave Dogon with Duncan—if you don't mind? Just in case he bothers the mermaids even more. We don't want him peeing at the edge of their lake and starting something."

"Nae bother," said Duncan. "I love dogs." He peered into the carrying case and raised an eyebrow. "Or dragons? Anyhoo, I love both."

"Good," said Alita. "Because Dogon *is* both."

"What does he eat?"

"Everything," said Alita. "Except mushrooms. He hates those."

"I'll take him back to my place for some food," said Duncan.

Duncan gave a wave and hopped into the cab of the van, gently laying Dogon's carrying case on the seat.

The rest of the group set off walking toward the loch.

CHAPTER 7

MORAG THE MERMAID

The loch was beautifully still and surrounded by rolling hills. The skies were clearing a little, and while it wasn't sunny yet, there were glimmers behind the clouds. Faith and the children stood on a pebbly shore.

"How do we get the mermaids to come and talk to us? Do we yell, like with Lizzie?" asked Kit.

Faith shook her head. "I think we need a gentler approach. Mermaids love music. Especially singing."

Kit frowned. "I don't think I should sing. Not unless we want to make them furious."

"Josh can sing," said Alita. "He's in his church choir."

"What should I sing, though?" asked Josh. "What kinds of songs do mermaids like?"

"Anything sad," said Faith. "But nothing mentioning sharks. Or fishermen."

In the end, Josh chose a song they'd learned at school, about an octopus. He had a nice voice, Kit thought. Quiet, but sweet.

Nothing happened for a moment. Then, ever so slowly, the surface of the loch began to ripple. Four figures rose up, with bare, scaly chests, their seal-like lower halves disappearing into the dark water. The mermaids had tangled hair that, Kit realized, was made of weeds. Their faces were covered in greeny-blue scales, and their eyes were huge and pale, with black slits for pupils. Kit noticed little lines down the sides of their necks.

"Ooh—gills!" whispered Alita. "They have gills!" She craned her neck to try to get a better look at the mermaids.

"And I think that one has a mer-beard!" said

Josh, nodding toward one of the mermaids, who had shorter hair and a hint of damp moss around his chin.

"Who disturbs our loch?" said the largest mermaid. Her voice was high and bubbling.

Faith stepped forward. "I am Faith Braithwaite, Wizard of Chatsworth, Keeper of the Library, my lady," she said. "We are here to request an audience."

"Why are you talking like that?" whispered Kit.

"It's how mermaids like to be spoken to," whispered Josh. "Shh."

"How does everyone know about mermaids and I don't?" asked Kit.

"Books," said Josh. "Shh."

"Well," said the mermaid. "Faith of Chatsworth, I am Morag of the Loch. Wizards are not welcome here. This loch is only for us now. No Lesser Nessies, no wizards, no mortals, just my merfolk."

"And fish," added one of the other mermaids.

"Yes," said Morag in a haughty voice. "And fish."

"Why don't you want to share the loch? You have for centuries." Faith's voice was perfectly

even, but there was a hint of irritation underneath it.

"Things have changed. The world is changing,"
said Morag. "It's mermaids for mermaids now. We
can't allow others to pollute our waters. We want
to be left alone."

She opened her pale eyes wider. When she spoke
next, her voice took on a strange tone. Kit felt the
sound deep inside her chest. It hurt. Part of her
wanted to turn and run.

"Go!" said the mermaid.

Kit turned to the others. They looked like they
wanted to be sick. Josh took a step back. Alita was
bent over, hands on her knees. Faith stood firm,
but a flicker crossed her face.

Morag was staring at them. "Why aren't you
leaving? I used my Tone of Power! You should be
gone by now!"

"Well, here we still are," said Faith. "And, since
you're being so rude, I won't bother addressing
you in the way you like. It seems your powers are

fading. Don't you wonder why we can approach your lake at all? Why we can see you? You should be able to hide yourselves when you don't want to be seen. Isn't that the mermaid way?"

"Wizard trickery!" Morag spat. But she didn't look entirely certain.

Faith went on. Her voice was level but steely. "Will you allow Lizzie to return? She's causing great harm with her sadness where she is now. She belongs here, with you."

"NO!" shrieked Morag. "Merfolk only!"

"Loch Lochy for the merfolk!" responded the others in a singsong chorus. Then they all began to chant, "Merfolk! Merfolk! HUMANS OUT! HUMANS OUT!"

"Well," said Faith. "I don't think we're going to have a sensible conversation here. Let's go. We can think of something else."

"YEAH, YOU'D BETTER RUN!" Morag shrieked after them. "Run on your weird flesh spikes, land-scuttlers!"

They walked rather than running away from the merfolk, but they waited until they were a good distance before they started talking.

"Wow. They were *mean*!" said Josh. "And my legs might be skinny, but 'flesh spikes' is a bit harsh!"

"They're *really* mean," agreed Kit. "I can see why Lizzie doesn't want to go back home."

"I want to know more about them, though," said Alita. She turned to Faith. "What do they look like on the bottom half? How can they talk if they have gills instead of lungs? Or do they have both?"

"What's their hair made of?" asked Josh.

"And what was that about a Tone of Power?" added Alita.

"And why isn't it working?" asked Josh.

"Honestly?" said Faith. "I'm embarrassed to say I haven't taken the time to study freshwater merfolk in detail, so I don't know as much as I'd like. At the Wizard Academy we mostly focused on the sea-dwelling kind, as they're in the majority all over the world. We'll have to do some more research," she added.

"You mean, we *get* to do more research," corrected Josh.

Kit stifled a groan.

Faith gave Josh an indulgent smile. "Duncan will be able to fill us in a little, but yes, we will need to read up more."

"Yay!" said Josh.

"I have a few answers, though. They *do* have gills and no lungs, I know that," said Faith. "And their hair is . . . a kind of underwater moss, I believe. They speak by vibrating certain small bones inside their necks. It's what gives their speech that weird shrill tone. Their Tone of Power is connected to that . . . and to their particular type of magic."

If that was what Faith called not knowing anything about a topic, Kit thought, she could fill nine hundred books with the topics she *did* know well.

Faith pulled the duradar out from her pocket. Its glow increased as she held it, swirling and whirling with milky light.

Faith held the ball up, close to her face, and spoke a spell: *"Parrhesia!"*

The ball flickered from milky white to a darker color. A picture was forming of a shady room full of books, and then Duncan's face came into view.

"Cool!" said Josh. He'd clearly forgiven the ball for not telling the future.

"Hello. Done already?" Duncan asked. His voice was perfectly clear, as though he were standing right next to them.

"Yes, and no luck," said Faith. "The mermaids were more or less how you found them last time. Though they didn't throw any rocks at least."

"Ah, I'm sorry they wouldn't help," said Duncan. "Though you'll be pleased to hear that Dogon has started to perk up, poor wee thing."

Alita gave a happy noise.

"Wait there a sec. I'll come and pick you up," said Duncan, and the duradar went dark.

They didn't have to wait long before Duncan's mobile library appeared over the nearest slope. It gave off no fumes as it drove along. Kit wondered if it was magic.

"Hop in!" called Duncan through the window. "The back doors are unlocked."

Alita was peering through the window of the van's cab. "Is Dogon in there with you?"

Duncan shook his head. "He's back at the house. Want to come and see how he's doing?"

Alita ran to the back of the van and was inside before he'd finished speaking.

CHAPTER 8

THE
WIZARD
HOLE

In the distance, they saw a hill. At least, it looked like a hill, but when Duncan drove them closer, Kit saw there was a large round green door in it.

Hills don't have doors, thought Kit.

Alita gasped. "It looks like a hobbit-hole!"

"*In a hole in the ground there lived . . .* a wizard," said Duncan.

Duncan pulled open the door, pausing on the doorstep and gesturing to the hill above it. "Having my home underground is very efficient in terms of keeping it heated. There are solar panels over the other side of the hill, and a wee wind farm." He pointed to the ground, where there was a patch of concrete with a little nozzle poking out of it. "That's where I charge the van when I'm at home."

"Ohhh, is the van electric? I thought it was magic," said Kit. She felt a bit disappointed.

"Powering a van by magic? That sounds exhausting! Do you know how much those things weigh?" said Duncan. "Now, come inside."

The home under the hill was very cozy. The ceiling was only a little taller than Duncan, and even Faith, who was quite a bit shorter than he was, had to duck to go through the circular door. The walls were covered with shelves, and every inch of the room seemed filled with furniture. Just then Dogon came barreling into the main living room from a back room, flying right into Alita and almost knocking her—and a shelf full of knickknacks—over. While he settled onto her shoulder, Alita stroked his fur and murmured relief into his ears. "You're OK!" she whispered.

Dogon did indeed look much healthier and was

clearly full of energy. He spent some of that energy trying to lick every inch of Alita's face with his little forked tongue. She held him at arm's length, giggling as his tongue lapped against empty air. "Sit!" she commanded, as she got over her giggle fit. Dogon fluttered to the floor and took a seat on a rug, looking up expectantly at Alita. "Good boy!" she said approvingly.

"Well, it seems that being away from Lizzie has done him good," said Faith. "Thanks for looking after him, Duncan."

"Nae bother," said Duncan. "He's a very pleasant little house guest, as long as you do a few fireproofing spells." He glanced at a singe mark on one of the curtains.

Faith sighed. "Sorry about that," she said. She raised a hand and muttered, *"Llosgi no, come back to before."* With a flick of her wrist, the curtains were as good as new.

Kit made a mental note to use that one. It would come in very handy with toast.

"Thanks!" said Duncan. "But, honestly, I've

done worse while experimenting with solar energy spells. In fact, this is the third house like this I've built. There's been some trial and error, let's say. With about as many errors as there were trials."

"You burned your house down?" asked Josh, looking worried.

"Twice," said Duncan.

"That's so cool!" said Kit.

Faith gave her a look.

"I mean . . . that's bad. I don't approve," Kit corrected.

As they settled down to make a plan, Duncan brought an apple pie out of the oven. "Brain food," he explained.

"We *are* in a hobbit-hole," said Josh approvingly. "It's like we're having second breakfast!"

Kit didn't know what second breakfast was, but she liked the sound of it. Homemade apple pie at eleven in the morning sounded even better. It smelled of cinnamon, and the hot, crusty pastry looked perfectly done.

"It smells so good!" said Alita.

Dogon immediately flew over to bother Duncan as he dished out the pie, until Alita whistled, and the little dragon dog retreated obediently to her side.

"That's better," she said, nestling Dogon into the gap between her legs and the side of the armchair.

The pie was delicious—sweet and hot, with a dollop of cream on top.

Whether it was the pie or the warmth of the snug little house, Kit started to feel very sleepy. The others chattered about magical creatures and apple pie and Dogon's naughty behavior as he begged for crumbs.

Kit's mind drifted. She thought about the mermaids and their angry faces and Morag's high voice. She thought about Dogon and how relieved she was that he was looking much better. She thought about the dark water of the loch.

Rising up through the water in her mind's eye, she saw a horrible face—no, a skull. A tiny, pointed skull, staring up at her from beneath the water. In the sockets of the skull glowed eerily blue eyes.

She heard
a voice saying,
"*Let us in.*"

A skeletal rat
leaped out at
her from the
water, right
at her face,
and she let out
a silent scream.

She sat up with a
start. There was a growling
sound beside her.

"You were snoring," said a voice. It was Alita.
"I don't think Dogon liked it much."

Kit realized she was slumped forward on her
arms, over the table. She sat up, blinking. Dogon
gave a disapproving snuffle.

"Sorry," she murmured.

"We didn't want to wake you. You looked so
peaceful," said Faith. "At least, until the end."

"Bad dream," muttered Kit.

"You've got apple pie in your hair," Josh pointed out.

Faith gave Kit a look of concern. "Is everything OK?"

Kit shrugged. "Just a bit sleepy."

Faith squinted at her. "If you're sure . . . then let's do some research. Find out more about what makes these mermaids tick."

Kit couldn't kick the feeling that something was watching her, though. Something with a pointed face and eyes of glassy blue. She thought she could hear the clattering of bones.

The three children were nestled amid gigantic piles of books on cushions in Duncan's little living room. Everyone was silent—even Dogon was calm, snoozing on a blanket in the corner.

Kit stared listlessly at her book. She kept trying to focus on the pages, but the words seemed to spin in front of her eyes. She didn't feel very well.

Her book was called *Mermaids: A Beginner's Guide*. But even that seemed too hard. She kept rereading the same passage about scales and gills.

Faith was sitting in a big armchair, reading a large volume called *Beyond the Mermaid: Water Peoples of the World*.

"Apparently, sea merfolk are sometimes known as saltfolk," she was telling them. "Freshwater merfolk, though—"

"Are they called freshfolk?" Josh asked.

"Don't interrupt," said Faith. She tapped the page. "Freshwater mermaids are all named after their individual bodies of water. So, riverfolk, lakefolk, and, in the case of Morag and the others, lochfolk. Although they often use 'mermaids' to mean any water people."

Josh scribbled some notes down about this. "What about streams? Are there streamfolk?"

"No, the water's too shallow," said Faith. "But there are quite a few groups of underwater lakefolk, especially in Mexico. The Cenogente."

Kit *really* wasn't feeling well now. Her vision was cloudy, and she had a churning feeling in her brain. She could feel tingles in her hands.

"I—" she began, but she couldn't finish before—

FWOOM!

Lightning filled the room. It took Kit a moment to realize that it was coming from her. Light was streaming from her fingertips. And . . .

FWOOM!

Suddenly she couldn't see.

"What's happening?" she gasped.

"Your eyes!" cried Alita. "They're . . . like lasers!"

Kit felt cool hands cupping the back of her head. Faith's voice spoke a few words: *"Ruo onwe gi!"*

Kit's vision returned, clear as ever. She noticed that the table on the other side of the room was smoking slightly from a large scorch mark in the middle.

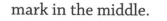

"Oops," she said. "Sorry!"

Alita and Josh rushed to her, looking her over, checking for injuries—and for laser eyes.

Faith was peering at her, worried. "Are you OK?"

"I think . . . yes.

Nothing hurts." She looked at her hands. "What *was* that?"

"Are you sure you're OK?" asked Alita.

Kit nodded. "What happened?" she asked.

"That was raw wild magic, bursting out of you," said Faith. She frowned. "I've only seen that once, at the Wizard Academy. It happened to a friend of mine during a very difficult spell. I didn't know it could happen spontaneously."

"I'm sorry about the table" was all Kit could think to say. She realized she was shaking. She'd never thought of herself as dangerous before. She looked at Alita and Josh. *What if this happens again and I hurt them?*

Alita and Josh were eyeing her cautiously. *Were* they afraid of her now? Well, perhaps they should be.

"What's wrong with her?" asked Josh. "Why did her magic burst out like that?"

The two children hovered around Kit, asking questions. She wanted to snap at them to go away and to stay away from her, in case she went all laser eyes again. Clearly, Duncan could tell she was worried.

"You've had a real shock. I'll make tea," he said tactfully. "Alita, Josh, can I have a hand with the cookies? Cookies are good for shock."

"But I want to know what's going on," said Josh.

"They're *very* heavy cookies," said Duncan, and led Josh and Alita to the kitchen.

Faith looked Kit in the eye. "Now. Let's see what's up." She pulled out her thaumometer and ran it up and down Kit. It lit up and let out a high-pitched noise that made Kit cover her ears. Faith pulled the thaumometer away, and the noise stopped.

"What's going on?" asked Kit. She felt her heart tha-thumping in her chest. "What's wrong with me?"

"Your wild magic levels are higher than the thaum can measure." Faith frowned so hard her eyebrows almost touched.

"I don't understand," said Kit. "I'm not near Lizzie now. Why is it getting worse? Dogon started going back to normal as soon as he was away from Lizzie."

"I don't know what's happening," said Faith.

"But this isn't the same as Lizzie's magic. It's something new. Still"—she brightened—"the spell I did on you just now should stop the magic from bursting out when you're just sitting there. So there's no immediate danger."

"Right," said Kit. Her voice was small and quiet. Knowing that her magic was out of control felt a little like having an extra limb that could move without her asking it to. Like having a big, swishy tail that smashed things every time she turned around. She didn't like it at all.

"Until we know what's causing this, you'd better be careful while doing magic," said Faith. "If you start feeling odd while doing a spell, stop whatever you're doing right away."

"So I don't have to stop doing magic while I'm like this?" said Kit.

"If I told you to stop doing spells, would you?" Faith asked, raising an eyebrow.

Kit looked away. "Uh . . ."

"I'd rather be realistic." Faith gave her an intense look. "Do magic, but take care."

Just then, they heard Josh yell from the next room. "It's on my feet!"

Alita let out a shriek of delight. "It's so cute! Look at it run!"

"Don't worry," came Duncan's voice. "It's just a rat."

"Just a RAT? JUST a RAT? On my actual feet?" Josh was screaming now.

"Rat?" Kit's antennae pricked up. "Where?"

Duncan and the others came back into the sitting room. "It's gone now. Fast little thing," said Duncan. "I think it was attracted by the smell of cookies."

He was carrying two trays—one with a teapot and some cups, the other piled with cookies.

"Made them myself," said Duncan. "The cookies, I mean. Not the rat. That arrived of its own accord."

Rats, thought Kit. *Where had she just seen rats?* She tried to grasp at the memory, but it scuttled into the back of her brain where she couldn't reach it.

"Duncan showed me the oven where he made the cookies," said Alita. "It's really cool. It's built down into the ground, and he's done a spell to tap into the earth's heat, so it doesn't use much energy."

"Can we do that back at the library?" asked Josh.

"Hmm," said Faith. "I think the council might have words if I start drilling holes to the earth's core."

When they finished their tea and cookies, they went back to their books.

"Oh!" said Alita, who was reading a book called *Deep Sea, Cold Loch: Wild Water Magic*. It was almost as big as she was, and her thin brown arms were clearly straining to keep the book upright as she held it. "This says that saltfolk draw their magic from the sea around them, but also from deep-sea monsters called . . ." She squinted at an unfamiliar word. "Kray-ens? Kray-kens?"

"Kraken. Of course!" said Faith. Her eyes lit up. "Why didn't I make the connection?" She shook her head. "I sometimes think I've forgotten more than most people learn in a lifetime. Wizards draw their power from dragons. Seafolk draw their power from krakens, so, obviously—"

"Lochfolk get theirs from Nessies!" said Alita and Josh at once.

"Oh, yeah. Obviously . . ." Kit was feeling sulky and left out. *Why doesn't my brain work fast like theirs do? Instead my brain just shoots out lasers and burns stuff.* She realized Faith was looking at her and tried to put on a more cheerful expression. "So what do we do now?"

"We just need to tell the lochfolk that Lizzie being away is the reason they're losing their powers," said Alita. "Then they'll let Lizzie come home!"

"Wouldn't they know that already?" said Josh. "Like . . . you know that wizards get their powers from dragons?"

"Not necessarily," said Faith. "Wizards read. Mermaids don't."

"I suppose books *would* get soggy in a loch," said Josh.

"So let's go and tell them that they need to let Lizzie come back," said Kit.

CHAPTER 9

THE QUIET VOICE

The mermaids rose out of the water at the sound of footsteps. Their scaly shoulders and knotty, weed-like hair glistened. Their huge eyes stared. Morag swam to the front of the group, keeping her head above water and her gaze fixed on Kit and her friends. Faith stood behind the children with Duncan, arms folded, observing.

"What do you want?" demanded Morag. "I told you, you can't bring your pet back here."

"She's not our pet," said Alita. "She's Lizzie."

"Well, she's not welcome," said Morag. "This is *our* loch, and it's going to stay that way."

"It's her loch, too!" said Alita.

"Also," said Kit, "aren't you wondering how we found you here? How we can see you?"

"Yeah," said Josh. "I bet you're trying to do your spells to push us away and keep yourself hidden, even now. But they're not working, are they?"

Morag frowned, wrinkling the scales of her forehead. "What would you know about magic, human child?"

"A lot," said Josh truthfully.

Alita was walking down to the bank of the loch.

"Get back!" said Morag. "You can't touch our water!"

Alita pulled off her shoe and sock and neatly dipped a toe in the water. "Yes I can," she said. "Your powers are fading even more than before." Then Alita looked back to Kit. "I don't suppose you'd . . ." She gestured to her wet foot.

Kit smiled, focused her mind on Alita's dripping toes for a second, and murmured, *"Sec!"*

"Thanks!" said Alita, waggling her now-dry toes before putting her sock and shoe back on.

"Are you all here just to go swimming, or do you have something to say?" asked Morag grumpily.

"Your powers are fading, as you can see," said Kit. "But we can help you get them back."

At that, the mermaids burst out laughing. "You?" Morag gestured to Faith. "Her, I'd believe, maybe. But you're a barely trained child wizard!"

"Actually, it was Alita and Josh who came up with the answer," said Kit.

"And we're not wizards at all," said Alita.

"We're very well trained though," said Josh. "Alita's level five on the piano and I can say hello in nine languages. *Bonjour! Privyet! Hallo! Sal—*"

"So spit it out," interrupted Morag. "What is this wonderful magical solution you're offering us?"

Alita explained. "You draw your wild magic from Lizzie, just as wizards draw theirs from dragons, and saltfolk draw theirs from krakens."

Morag looked a little hesitant. "We do?" Then she shook her head. She appeared to be listening to something. "Doesn't matter! This loch is ours! Merfolk only!"

"Merfolk for merfolk!" chorused the other mermaids. Their eyes seemed glazed over, Kit thought.

"But if you want to keep yourselves to yourselves, you need your powers," said Alita. "If you allow Lizzie to return to the loch, your powers will return. And you'll be able to hide yourselves from prying human eyes again. And no one will be able to dip their toes in your loch." Alita waved her foot to reinforce her point.

"Of course, you don't *have* to let Lizzie return," said Kit. "We could leave you alone now and keep Lizzie with us . . . and you could grow weaker and weaker until every day ends up being a human pool party in the loch. I bet you'd like to share your loch with a giant inflatable, wouldn't you? And lots of screaming toddlers in floaties?"

"And you'll probably get found by scientists coming for a swim and end up in a zoo," said Josh. Then he thought about this. "Well, it would probably be an aquarium, not a zoo."

"I don't think you need to be quite so accurate

in your threats, Josh," said Faith, trying not to smile.

Morag said nothing. She just narrowed her round eyes.

Kit glanced at the others. "Perhaps we're wasting our time here? Let's leave these mermaids alone. Well, not alone for *long*."

"Wait!" said Morag. "Don't be hasty." She held up a webbed hand. "Let me talk to my people."

Kit nodded and folded her arms, as if she were impatient to leave. "I'll give you a minute. Then we're going."

The mermaids clustered together in a circle. Their voices were too low to catch, so Kit put a finger to her lips and whispered, *"Broadcast the quiet, ymhelaethu!"*

". . . we have to let the Lesser Nessie back," Morag was saying. "Better to have Lizzie in our lake than a gaggle of humans!"

"Agreed," said one of the others. "I don't want to end up in an aquarium! They might put us in the same tank as a shark! Or worse, a really annoying octopus!"

"That's settled, then," said Morag. "We bring Lizzie back."

She turned to Kit and began to swim forward. She opened her mouth to speak. But then another voice rang out instead. A high, strange voice, which sounded as if it came from far away.

"*Don't give in, Morag,*" it said. "*If you do as we say, we will give you power again. A power more ancient than human wizardry. We will protect your loch. Don't give in just yet . . .*"

Morag's face froze. She looked as though she were suddenly very far away. She hesitated.

Kit didn't like the look of this. "Well, what's your answer?" she said.

Morag didn't reply. She was waiting for something. For the voice to speak again?

"Do not waver. This loch is yours. Don't let that beast return. We will protect you from outsiders. This loch is for merfolk only, remember that. When we return, you will have more power than ever. Trust us . . ."

Kit looked at her friends. They were just staring at Morag, looking confused.

"Are you hearing this?" she asked them. She looked at Faith.

"No, I can't hear anything," said Faith. Her forehead gathered into a frown of concentration. "What can you hear?"

"A voice. Or maybe lots of voices. They sound . . . familiar. They're saying something about giving the mermaids power . . . protecting them from outsiders," Kit said. She blinked, trying to recall what the voice had said. But it was already fading from her mind.

Faith spoke a spell that Kit didn't recognize, then listened. "Still nothing." She sighed. "Somehow it's a voice that only Kit can hear."

"Me and the mermaids," said Kit. She pointed at Morag, who was staring into space. "She's waiting for it to speak again."

"Hmm," said Faith thoughtfully. "That's odd."

The voice—or many voices—appeared again in Kit's head. This time, the voice felt closer, as though it were coming from deep inside her brain. It was as loud and jolting as an alarm clock.

"Only the child can defeat us. Send her away."

Kit blinked for a moment. What *was* that voice?

"The answer is no," said Morag, turning to Faith and the children. Her face had a faraway look and her voice sounded almost robotic. "Go away. We can look after our own. Merfolk for merfolk!" she cried, slapping her scaly chest with her webbed palm.

"Merfolk for merfolk!" the others chimed in.

And they dived under the water, tails flapping in the air, and were gone.

"The voices you heard . . . what were they like?" asked Faith as the water became still again.

Kit shivered. "Something . . . I can't describe them. They were very high and very far away. It was as though they were inside my mind. They felt . . ." She shook her head. There were no words for what hearing that voice felt like. She just knew she never wanted to hear it again.

"They said I was the only one who could defeat them," she said.

At that, Faith looked worried. "I see," she said.

"I don't like the sound of that," said Josh. "If a gang of evil wizards thinks Kit is the only one who can defeat them . . . Well, in books, evil wizards who are afraid of children try to kill those children. Or, at the very least, imprison them forever in a dungeon made of burning-hot glass, like Malvolio did in book one of Danny Fandango."

Kit gulped. She didn't like the sound of either option.

"We don't know they're evil wizards. The voices, I mean," Duncan pointed out. "We just know that they're controlling the mermaids. Making them keep Lizzie away. For some reason . . ." His dark eyebrows knitted together, thoughtful.

"How do we find out who they are?" asked Kit.

"How do we *stop* them from controlling the mermaids? And get them out of my head? It's *my* head; I don't like having other people talking in it! Especially not spooky voices that are out to get me!"

Duncan stroked his beard. "I have an idea. Let's go see a friend of mine. It's walking distance to her place, but quicker to drive. She might have a few ideas about who's behind this."

"Who's your friend?" asked Kit.

"You'll see," said Duncan. He beckoned them all to follow him.

"Where's he taking us?" Kit asked Faith as they headed to the mobile library van.

"No spoilers," said Faith with a grin.

Duncan drove them through the hills, along winding little bumpy roads. Kit thought it was a shame to be stuck in the back of the van without a view. But when they stopped and got out of the mobile library, she gasped. She was standing in the midst of a towering forest of white poles. A *whomp whomp whomp* noise filled the air.

"It's a wind farm," said Duncan. "It's how we get our power out here, aside from the solar panels." He looked up at the sun, which was high in the midday sky but half-covered with clouds. "We don't get a lot of sun," he admitted.

Near the base of one of the gigantic wind turbines, where the van was parked, was a little post with an outlet in it. Duncan pulled a cord out of a flap in the back of his van and plugged it in.

"Now, we can leave that charging while we go and pay my friend a visit."

Kit looked around. There were no buildings, and definitely no people, anywhere nearby.

"Are we going to walk?" Josh asked in a worried voice. He looked down at his pristine white sneakers, then at the mossy, muddy ground, with the expression of someone being asked to throw a puppy into a shark tank.

"Walk where?" said Duncan. "We're already here." He opened his palm and held it up to the sky. *"Foss gell cheh nah hed be owl."*

The earth where they stood began to sink, ever so slowly.

Kit felt Josh grip her arm. "Whoa! Earthquake!" he said. "No, wait. Spell. Don't panic."

"I wasn't panicking," said Kit. "And you're hurting my arm."

"Sorry," said Josh as he let go.

They sank into the ground. At first they seemed to be traveling down a shaft with earthen walls, but soon the walls began to fade, and they found themselves in a vast space. The little tuft of grass they stood on floated down through the air like a grassy magic carpet.

Below them came a faint glow of green. A familiar glow.

Kit peeked over the edge of the tuft of moss that was carrying them down and down and down. The green glow grew stronger.

"It's a book wood!" she gasped.

"It's even bigger than the one at our library!" said Josh.

"It's the only wizard library for miles around," said Duncan. "So it can expand as far as it likes."

Alita was staring in silent awe. Finally, as their tuft of moss touched down lightly on the ground of the book wood, she said, with a voice trembling in excitement, "Duncan, does this mean we're going to meet your dragon?"

CHAPTER 10

SHADOWS AROUND A FLAME

The dragon's cave was a lot like Draca's lair, although it was much bigger. The dragon was bigger, too. The hum of its magic was not the familiar warmth of Draca's power, but something colder. Something . . . older, Kit thought, though she wasn't sure how she knew this.

The dragon's scales were red, whereas Draca's were green. Its face was broader and its snout was shorter. Its wings were vast, spread out on either side of its body like the wings of a plane.

"Shall we go and say hello?" asked Duncan.

He didn't have to ask twice.

The children were already by the dragon's side, holding hands with Faith. Kit looked to Faith, who looked to Duncan, and he nodded. Kit put her hand on the dragon. So did Faith. So did Duncan. Then everything went black.

In the dragon's dream, the cave became a beach. The dragon was spread on a giant beach chair wearing sunglasses and drinking a fruity drink with pineapple bits in it. A whale leaped out of the bright-blue ocean and crashed back down, splashing them all.

"Ah," said Duncan. "I've been reading her a lot of travel books lately. She's clearly been enjoying them. This is Nath," he added, gesturing to the dragon.

Nath was watching them curiously over her sunglasses. "Humans," she said. "Humans who aren't Duncan. That's unusual."

She lay back on the beach chair for a moment, letting out a sigh that blossomed from between her lips in a slow cloud of flame. "Humans are so new. I remember the time before. Now *that* was something."

"The time before humans?" asked Alita.

"Oh, so long before humans," said Nath. "A time when magic was everywhere, in the open, unafraid. A time before the masters came and made us fall asleep."

"The Dragon Masters," murmured Faith. "The ones who killed the dinosaurs. Ancient wizards. Ancient, *evil* wizards. As the stories go, they're the ones who made the dragons sleep, to harness their power. And once, they killed a dragon, hoping to absorb its power. It didn't work out so well for them—or for the dinosaurs."

"But wait . . ." Josh was frowning so deeply that Kit thought he might fold his entire forehead in two. "How can evil wizards have killed the dragon that killed the dinosaurs?" asked Josh. He threw up his hands in disbelief. "Surely you know that the dinosaurs died out millions of years before humans arrived? There can't have been wizards then!"

"Did I say they were *human* wizards?" asked Faith.

Josh's eyes widened. "WOW. If they weren't human, what were they?"

"Nobody knows," said Faith.

Kit felt that was enough about ancient wizard history.

"We were wondering if you could help us," she said to Nath. "We're here to help Lizzie come home. Some mermaids are being controlled by a spell, and they've chased Lizzie away. Do you know who's controlling them?"

At the edges of the beach, shadows began to gather. A storm filled the sky, and Nath seemed to shrink. There was a skitter of movement out of the corner of Kit's eye. She shuffled closer to her friends. "I have been having dark dreams," said Nath. "Of dead things. Of ancient things. Of bones. Of rats."

At that moment, a rat scuttled over Kit's feet. She yelled at the top of her lungs.

"Sorry," said Nath. "I was thinking of the rats again and . . . they appeared. When I think of a thing, I make it real. For you are in my mind. In my dream."

Faith, Duncan, and the children came closer to the dragon.

"Do the rats you're seeing have anything to do with who's controlling the mermaids?" asked Faith.

That reminded Kit of something, at the edges of her brain. Blue eyes. Skeletal cheeks. But she couldn't grasp the image, and it melted.

The dragon took a deep breath and blew out smoke rings before she answered.

"I can't see them clearly. The spellmakers. They're on the edges of my vision. They're long ago and far away. They're dancing like shadows around a flame." Nath looked at Kit. "And you're the flame."

She threw back her head and let out a terrifying roar. "Go away! You're bringing trouble! GO AWAY!"

Kit started to back away.

"Nath! Why are you being like this?" asked Duncan. He turned to Kit. "Sorry, she's usually so gentle . . . but I think we should go."

"Goodbye, Nath," said Faith.

The world went black once more.

CHAPTER 11

THE
POWER
OF
THREE

I don't think your dragon likes me very much," said Kit when they got back to Duncan's house.

"Don't mind her," said Duncan. "She's just scared. I'm sorry she wasn't more helpful. Dragons can be vague at the best of times, but something's really got her spooked."

"What did she mean about me being a flame?" asked Kit. She pictured the lasers coming out of her eyes and shuddered.

"Nath doesn't always speak in ways that humans can follow," said Duncan. "She's very old and has slept a long time. But I think she meant that whoever or whatever is doing this is drawn to you. Like a moth is drawn to a flame."

Kit realized that Faith was looking at her intently. "What do you think it means, Kit? Dig deep."

Kit tried to focus. She thought about the voice and how it sounded. She thought about the lake. Then, for an instant, her mind cleared. The dream she'd forgotten bubbled up to the surface of her brain.

"Rats," she murmured. "I think that's what I dreamed of, when I fell asleep after we had our apple pie."

"At second breakfast, you mean," corrected Josh.

"You dreamed of rats?" asked Alita, giving Josh a look.

"I think it was a rat's skull," said Kit, trying to picture the details of her dream. "With glowing blue eyes. Then this skeleton jumped out of the water at me, and I woke up. What does it mean?" she asked.

Faith shrugged. "That's the trouble with dreams. They're not like books. They never come with footnotes to explain their meanings. Sometimes they don't mean anything. But when a dragon and a wizard have the same dream . . ." She trailed off, looking thoughtful. "That's not a coincidence."

"It could be a prophecy," piped up Josh. "Maybe Kit is seeing the future in her sleep?"

"So my future involves dead rats? Nice," said Kit.

"Prophecies aren't as straightforward as that," said Faith. "But hopefully Kit hasn't developed a talent for prophecy. That would make life too predictable. Who wants to know what's coming? Isn't half the fun of life finding out?"

"I don't like surprises," said Josh. "They make me jump."

A moment later he pointed at the leather-bound book on his lap, which was so big he had to stretch to turn the pages. "I've found something."

From where Kit was sitting, she could feel a hum of magic buzzing through the book on Josh's lap.

"I've found a spell that breaks mind-control spells, and it says you don't need to know who's done the spell, just who it's been done *to*." He looked up in triumph.

Faith took the book from Josh. "Good eye, Josh. This should do perfectly."

Josh beamed.

"Ah, it's a three spell," said Faith.

"Three what?" asked Alita.

Josh put his hand up. "Oh, I know!"

Faith raised an eyebrow. "We're not in school, Josh."

Josh lowered his hand. "Sorry," he said. "The spell needs three wizards to perform it."

"Right. Good thing we're all here, then. We three can perform the spell," said Faith, gesturing at Duncan and Kit.

Kit's heart soared.

"We'll keep an eye on you in case of any more . . . explosions," said Faith. "Duncan and I can help you stay in control and keep you steady."

Kit's heart de-soared.

"And I can help with the hand gestures if you can't remember the order of them," said Josh.

"What should I do?" asked Alita eagerly.

"You could take Dogon for a walk," Kit suggested.

"Keep him away from where we're doing the spell so he doesn't distract us."

Alita's face fell. "Oh," she said in a small voice. "That's fine. I'll take Dogon now and meet you all back here."

"Wait, Alita," said Kit, sensing that she'd done something wrong but not sure what it was.

"Bye!" said Alita. "Come, Dogon!" she said, then whistled. Dogon fluttered toward her.

"Come on," said Faith. "Let's go free some mermaid minds."

They arrived near the lake and made sure to stop where they weren't so close that the mermaids would spot them, but close enough for the magic to take hold. Duncan handed the book to Josh, open at the right page.

"OK, now we have our hands free to gesture," said Faith. "Thanks, Josh."

"Happy . . . to . . . help . . ." said Josh, gritting his teeth. "This book . . . is . . . quite . . . heavy."

"We'll say the spell quickly, then!" said Kit.

They began the spell. The words were simple and the gestures were all ones Kit had used before. With a spell book this powerful, no fancy gestures or complicated phrases were needed. Josh mouthed the words alongside her all the same, which she found half-annoying and half-comforting.

"*Liberay hugur, break . . .*" she chanted with Faith and Duncan.

As they spoke, Kit felt a power building inside her. Was it the spell taking hold? Was it working? The hum of magic grew stronger and stronger . . . until, with a bright-green flash and a deafening *BANG!* she felt a flood of magic rush through her body, from her toes through her chest to the top of her head. She was blown through the air and fell heavily onto her hands and knees.

Out of the corner of her eye, Kit thought she saw movement. Something skittering away into the heather. She saw the flash of a pink tail. Then another. And another.

Then, while she knelt dazed on the ground, she heard three voices begin to chant again. Duncan, Faith, and . . . Josh.

"Liberay hugur, break . . . glee matsy angina. Liberay!"

Kit looked up at the others, blinking in surprise. "Josh?"

Duncan offered her a hand, but she scrambled to her feet on her own.

"What happened?" she asked, still feeling dazed.

"Your power burst out midway through. A more extreme version of what happened earlier. Josh finished the spell for you."

Josh beamed. "Well, everyone knows that you never leave a spell half-finished!" he said. "And since Kit fell over, I thought I should try. Even though I'm not a wizard, so it was a bit dangerous." He looked a little pale, like he was only just realizing what he'd done.

Duncan slapped him on the back. "Good lad. You made the right call."

Kit glanced down at her hands. They looked normal. But she felt very drained. She wobbled slightly on her feet. "What's wrong with me?" she whispered. "Am I . . . broken?"

"No, of course not," said Faith. She put a hand on Kit's shoulder. "I'm sorry. I shouldn't have asked you to do the spell while you were like this."

Kit felt like crying. She wanted to ask, *What if I'm always like this? What if I can never do spells again?*

Duncan came over to her. "You look a bit green," he said. "Are you OK?"

"I think so," said Kit.

"Would you like to go and lie down on my sofa?" he offered.

"Maybe you should eat a cookie?" suggested Josh. "That helped last time you went a bit . . ." He gestured an explosion around his head. "Boom!"

Kit shook her head. *I ruined the spell,* she thought. *My magic is out of control. I can't be trusted. Josh had to risk himself because I failed.*

"I'm fine," she said. "I might go and see if I can find Alita. Will you be here still?"

"Yup," said Faith. "Don't worry. You go and clear your head."

Kit looked down at her hands again, biting her lip a little. Tears were pricking at the edges of her eyes.

She rushed off before the pricking tears risked coming in a flood. She walked quickly over the purple heather, breathing in the wet smell of the land. However fast she walked, her mind whirred faster. *What if my magic's broken? What if I'm dangerous? What if Lizzie can never come home, and Dogon will have to stay here, and it's all my fault?*

Midthought, she saw a shape in the sky just over the hill. She broke into a run and, getting closer, saw that it was Dogon. Alita was sitting on a stone, watching the creature with a distant look on her face.

"Alita!" Kit called.

Alita turned and waved. Dogon fluttered down onto her shoulder.

"Have you finished the spell?" asked Alita as Kit drew closer. "Are the mermaids back to normal?"

Kit shook her head. "My magic went wrong again and messed everything up," she said. "Josh finished the spell to stop things from getting worse."

"Josh is clever like that," said Alita. She didn't sound entirely pleased about it. Kit took a seat on the cool stone next to her friend. They both watched Dogon for a moment. Then Alita spoke up.

"It's going to be OK, you know. I'm sure Faith will figure out what's up with your magic."

"But what if she can't? What if it's permanent?" The thought was terrible.

"Well, even if your magic is going wrong, at least you *have* magic," said Alita in a quiet voice.

Kit turned to her friend and noticed for the first time that her eyes were all red and puffy. She'd been crying. "Oh, Alita, are you OK?"

Alita shrugged and tried to smile. "I just feel . . . like there's nothing I can do to help Dogon. What if he can never go home? And Lizzie. What if she's stuck in our lake forever? I want to help, but I don't have your magic. I don't have Josh's brains. And . . ." She was starting to cry again. "I just feel like I'm in the way!"

"You're not in the way!" said Kit, almost angry with Alita for thinking that. "You're my best friend!"

"But I can't do anything special," said Alita. Her mouth went small and tight, and Kit worried she might start crying again.

"Well, do you think I want to be friends with people because they have special powers or genius brains?" Kit asked. "Are you friends with *me* because I have magic powers?"

Alita frowned. "Well, no. We're friends because I like you." She picked up one of her braids and started playing with it. "I feel like you're tricking me into feeling better."

"Is it working?" asked Kit.

"I think it is," said Alita. She broke into a grin. "Kit Spencer, your magic powers may not be working right now, but your cheering-up powers are on fire."

Kit smiled. She realized that cheering up Alita was making *her* feel better. That was a kind of magic, too.

A shadow passed over her friend's face again.

"I'm still worried," said Alita. "I want to make it all OK again!"

"Me too," said Kit. "But at least Dogon doesn't seem worried!"

"No, he looks like he's having a great time," agreed Alita. "I think he likes it out here."

Above them, Dogon was doing loop-the-loops, cruising on his back on the air currents at the top of each loop. As he did, he put his little paws behind his head like someone floating in the sea.

They watched Dogon for a moment, until he swooped down to land and trotted off over the hill.

"Dogon, where are you going?" called Alita. The girls got up from the stone and followed him. When they caught up, he was digging in the heather. Then he put his little snout down and snapped something up with a chirrup and a chomping sound.

"What have you got there?" Alita asked. She reached her hand out, and Dogon backed away with a naughty look in his eye. "Oh, you want me to chase you, do you?"

Dogon kept backing away with a playful growl. Just as Alita started to run toward him to start the game of chase, Dogon let out a horrible whining sound and curled up into a sad little furry ball.

"Dogon!" cried Alita, running to him and kneeling to take the creature's head in her arms. "I think he's got something stuck in his throat," she said. She put her fingers into Dogon's mouth and fished out a bone. As soon as it was free, Dogon gave a little snort, puffing out smoke and uncurling himself. Then he started to lick Alita's hand gratefully, nuzzling close to her.

As Kit leaned down to pat Dogon, Alita gave a hiss. "OUCH!" She hurriedly dropped the bone

that she'd been holding. On her palm was a strange mark, like a little curly X. "Oh," said Alita. "It doesn't hurt anymore but . . . that's odd."

Kit peered at the mark. "I think that's magical," she said. "That's not just a burn mark or something. It's too . . . curly."

She knelt to look at the bone. It looked perfectly ordinary, like something you'd see left over after you'd eaten roast chicken for Sunday dinner.

Alita knelt beside her. "I think that's from a mammal. It might be an upper leg bone."

"You know weird stuff," said Kit approvingly. "Now, we need to take this back to Faith to look at."

"I don't know," said Alita. "Maybe we shouldn't get close to it, after . . ." She held up her palm. The X was starting to fade, but Kit could still see its faint outline.

"Can you do a spell to lift it?" suggested Alita.

"But . . . my magic might still be going wild. What if it goes wrong and I shoot flames out of my eyeballs again and hurt you?"

"It's fine." Alita shrugged. "I'll stand way back. If anyone gets their eyebrows singed, it'll be you." She smiled.

Kit swallowed and prepared herself for a simple lifting spell.

"Levantar!" she said, gesturing at the bone to lift in the air. It wobbled for a moment, then slowly raised itself upward. There was no green flash, no bang, and nothing went wrong. Kit kept her arm raised, holding the bone out in front of her, hovering in the air, just to be safe. Dogon kept back, sitting on Alita's shoulder.

"You did it!" said Alita.

"Now I just need to keep focusing on it until we get back to the others."

They walked quietly toward the lake.

When Faith saw them coming with the floating object in front of them, she did a double take. "What . . . is that?" she asked, breaking into a jog, her locs swaying and her jewelry jangling.

"Don't touch it!" warned Kit.

"Noted!" said Faith. She spoke a spell of her own,

pulling the object through the air toward her with a swiping gesture.

Duncan came to look at it. "Looks like rat bone. Although it's about ten times too big."

Josh came over to join Kit and Alita while Faith and Duncan inspected the bone, which was hovering between them now.

"What did we miss here?" asked Kit.

"Not much," said Josh. "They've just been trying a few spells to figure out what went wrong, but nothing yet. Where did you find the bone?"

"We didn't," said Alita. "Dogon did." Dogon was a little way off, rolling around in the heather.

"What's that on your hand?" Josh asked.

Alita showed him her fading cross.

Josh gasped. "Alita, I know that mark! I've read about it in one of the books in the stacks. You need to show it to Faith *now*."

"Why?" asked Alita, massaging her palm, her eyes suddenly wide with fear.

"Because that's the mark left by a spell," said Josh. "That bone is cursed."

CHAPTER 12

THE CURSED BONE

There was a lot of fuss after that. Duncan and Faith did a cleansing spell on Alita and Dogon on the spot. "That should tide you over until we can get you home," said Duncan. They were striding across the heather toward his underground home. "I have some herbs there that I can use to wipe away the effects of the curse on anyone who's touched it."

When they got back, Faith busied herself with creating a safe place to put the bone, and Duncan brewed a healing potion.

After a few minutes, he returned with two

eggcups full of a stinky browny-green goop, hand-ing one to each of the girls.

"I didn't touch the bone! I feel fine," objected Kit.

"You were near it for longer than the rest of us, though. Best to be on the safe side," said Duncan. He made her take the eggcup.

"I don't have to be on the safe side, do I?" asked Josh, edging away from them on the sofa. "I like the dangerous side, where I don't have to drink that."

"You should be fine." Duncan laughed.

"Good," said Josh. "Because it smells worse than the sewage treatment plant behind my uncle's house. It smells like something that's been living at the back of the fridge for a year, boiled in vomit."

"Can you stop describing it?" begged Alita.

"Yeah, we're the ones who actually have to drink it!" growled Kit.

"Sorry," said Josh, looking more relieved than sorry.

Kit peered into her eggcup and gave a sniff. Josh was right. It was foul. She immediately regretted having a nose.

"It might smell horrible," said Duncan. "But believe me, drinking this is a thousand times better than whatever might happen when a curse kicks in."

Kit and Alita exchanged glances. "Same time?" suggested Kit.

Alita nodded. "Hold your nose!" she said.

They both did, and knocked back their potions.

"DISGUSTING!" Kit choked out.

"Urrrrrr!" Alita coughed.

Dogon, meanwhile, was lapping hungrily at a saucer full of his potion.

"Why is Dogon's so tasty?" asked Kit.

"You can't persuade a pup that something's for their own good, so you have to make their potions tasty," said Duncan.

"Remind me to be less easy to persuade next time," said Kit.

"Let's hope there's *no* next time," said Faith. She had crossed the room to join them on the squishy chairs and sofa. She held a glowing box that appeared to be made out of light. With a gesture, it rose into the air, rotating slowly. It was almost solid-looking, but Kit could just about make out a little white object at its heart. The bone.

"This will stop it from doing any harm," said Faith, gesturing to the box. "It's sort of a magical trap. To keep the bone from cursing anyone."

"Phew!" said Josh.

"So we're definitely safe?" asked Alita. She was looking down at her hand nervously. Dogon, who'd finished his potion, hopped up onto the sofa beside her and rested his furry muzzle in her lap.

"Completely," said Duncan. "Curse-free."

"So," said Faith. "Should we run some tests on this bone?"

"What kind of tests?" asked Josh.

"I thought I'd try a backtrace spell, to see where the spell came from that cursed this bone. Perhaps it's the same group of wizards controlling the mermaids."

"What's a backtrace spell?" asked Kit.

"Oh, oh, I know this!" said Josh. He didn't put his hand up, but Kit could tell that he really wanted to.

Faith nodded at him. Her mouth was twitching

toward a smile, but she stayed serious. "Go on."

"It's like . . . you know on police TV shows, where the police are on the phone with a bad guy, and they try to keep the bad guy on the phone so they can use computers to check where the bad guy's calling from? It's like that, but without police or computers and with magic. It's a spell to find out where a spell's coming from and going to," he finished.

"Definitely no computers or police," said Faith. "But that's it exactly. It uses scrying magic. Let me show you," Faith went on. "Duncan, do you have a map of the area?"

"Aye." He got up and went to rustle through some papers on a shelf. Josh took out his notebook as Faith explained what they would be doing.

> Scrying magic is for finding out information. I remember it by thinking about "prying." My grandma always says "Don't pry" when she wants me to mind my own business.

Kit sat up eagerly, ready to learn a new spell.

She wasn't disappointed.

When Duncan laid a map down on the coffee table, Faith began.

"To the keld, connect!"

Faith gestured to the bone in its shining cage, then moved her hands out to the side, then directly to the sky, then to the ground. A hum began deep in the ground, rising up through Kit, through the room, through the earth. The bone began to spin in its cage, faster and faster, until a flash of red light shot out from it like a laser beam. It hit the map, highlighting a spot in the middle without burning the paper.

"The loch," said Josh. "It's coming from the loch." He frowned. "Are the wizards who cursed the bone in the loch? Like, in scuba gear or something?"

The light faded. Faith shook her head. "No, they're not. Because the curse isn't coming from the loch."

"But the light from the bone went to the loch. Doesn't that mean the wizard who cursed this bone is there?"

"No," said Faith. "Because if that were the case, the light would have begun on the map and spread to the bone. This went the other way around."

Kit didn't know what any of this meant. "What?" she said.

"So . . . the curse isn't going from a wizard to the

bone?" said Alita thoughtfully. "It's going from the bone to the loch?"

Kit felt the cogs turn in her brain. The thoughts fell into place with satisfying clicks. "There aren't any evil wizards doing this," she said. "It's the bone itself. The bone is controlling the mermaids!"

CHAPTER 13

THE ANCIENT CURSE

A bone spreading a curse," said Alita. "That's creepy! I wonder who cursed it?"

"And how do we break the curse?" asked Kit.

"Before we can get any answers, we need to know what kind of curse we're dealing with. We'll need supplies," said Faith.

"Like herbs and stuff?" asked Alita.

"Magic potions?" asked Josh.

"No!" said Faith. "Food. I'm starving! It's definitely past lunchtime, and I can't think on an empty stomach."

"Me too!" said Kit. She looked at her watch. It

was two thirty! No wonder her stomach was almost eating itself. Apple pie, cookies, and disgusting anti-curse juice were *not* enough to fuel a growing wizard into the afternoon.

Duncan made some cheese sandwiches with cheddar from a local farm, fresh butter, and bread he'd baked himself. Faith made a drink called chocolate tea, which involved grating little balls of chocolate that looked like dinosaur eggs, together with fresh nutmeg and cinnamon, then melting it all together on the stove with thick, creamy condensed milk. It was so delicious, Kit let out little yelps as she drank it.

Then they set to work.

Faith used her thaumometer to measure the magic coming off the bone. Its gem glowed a bright yellow, vibrating slightly as Faith held it. She widened her eyes. "Strong," she said. "And it's definitely mind magic. A control curse."

As she passed the device back and forth in front of the floating bone, Faith frowned. She looked at the thaumometer and shook it a few times.

"What's wrong?" asked Kit.

"I'm measuring the magical decay. That is, how old the curse is. And it's older than it should be. I think there might be something wrong with my thaum."

"How old is it saying it is?" asked Kit.

"About . . . I don't know

exactly, but more than . . . fifty million years."

"Someone made this curse fifty million years ago?" Kit's brain boggled at the idea.

"Well, not someone human," said Josh. "There weren't humans then."

Kit remembered something. She turned to Faith. "You said the Dragon Masters were wizards . . . but they weren't human." She pointed at the bone. "Could they have made this curse? Back before they killed the dinosaurs? And themselves?"

"Oh." Faith went over to the bone, peering into its glass case. "Kit, I think you're right." Her face was full of wonder. "We could be looking at one of the last spells the Dragon Masters cast before they died."

"This is a piece of wizard history," said Duncan. "It belongs in the Museum of Magic! Or it will once we've broken the curse."

"Seriously," said Faith. "I know a curator who will literally scream when I tell him about this."

"Dogon's a clever little historian for finding it," said Alita, giving the creature a few scratches behind his ears.

"I wonder what triggered the curse," said Duncan. "The bone must have been here for a very long time. Why did it start affecting the mermaids now?"

"Maybe one of them found it in the loch," suggested Alita. "Like Dogon did. And threw it out of the water without realizing what it was?"

"But by then they'd all touched it, and it was too late!" said Kit. She could just picture the grumpy mermaids throwing away the bone, slowly starting to fall under the thing's cursed spell.

Josh was pacing up and down, his giant brain clearly throbbing with ideas. "So the mermaids triggered the curse . . . and then the bone started to control them. Why did it make them chase Lizzie away?"

"And why did it say I'm the only one who can stop it?" said Kit. "Why's it talking to the mermaids? Can curses talk?"

"Good question!" said Faith.

"I asked a good question?" asked Kit.

"Don't sound so surprised," said Faith.

"It can't just be a simple curse," said Duncan. "The bone seems to be . . . thinking."

This was all getting to be a bit much for Kit. "How can a bone think?"

Faith peered at the bone. "I believe—though I'm not sure—that the Dragon Masters bound a little bit of their essence to this bone. So when they died, their minds stayed behind. It's called a will curse. The most powerful of all curses. And, clearly, the longest-lasting."

"Millions of years long!" said Josh, impressed.

Kit blinked. This hurt her brain. "I still don't get why they're controlling the mermaids."

"Neither do I," said Faith. "And I don't like not knowing."

"What can we do? We still have to break the curse," said Alita, "or the mermaids will keep Lizzie away, and Dogon will never be able to go home!"

"Not to mention what's probably happening back at home the longer Lizzie stays there," muttered Faith.

Alita looked worried. "Will everyone back at home be OK?"

Faith waved off her worry. "Oh, it won't be

dangerous. It will just be . . . awkward to explain to the Wizards' Council."

Alita nodded, relieved.

"What breaks curses like this?" asked Kit.

"Wild magic," said Faith. "Wildness breaks up the will of the curse caster and splits it apart from the cursed object."

"Oh! So can we use Nath's magic?" asked Kit.

Faith shook her head. "A dragon's magic would be too raw, too fierce. It would hurt the mermaids."

"We can use the wild magic of nature!" suggested Duncan. "In every blade of grass, there's a tiny trace of wild magic. And in every ant and every animal." He waved his hand at the round windows, looking out on the rolling heather.

"Hmm," said Faith, thinking. "We need to focus the wild magic in nature on the bone, and on the mermaids, to break the curse."

"This book says crystals are good for focusing magic," said Josh. "Do you have any?"

"Yes, but none big enough," said Duncan.

"I have a question," said Alita, who'd been silent

for a while. "Do we have to do a spell to gather up all the wild magic? Can't we just gather creatures instead? And take them to the mermaids? Would that work?"

"Genius!" cried Faith. "That, Alita, is a stroke of genius!"

Kit thought Josh looked ever so slightly annoyed at that. But Alita's face lit up like a star. "Really?" she said.

"How do we get animals to gather, though?" asked Josh. "Like, use a sheepdog?"

"Don't worry about that," said Duncan. "I have my ways. Alita, perhaps you and Kit could help me?"

"Excellent," said Faith. "Then Josh and I will find exactly the right spell to channel that wild nature magic and break the curse."

"So I don't have to go and chase after ants and stuff?" asked Josh.

"No chasing. Just reading," Faith replied.

"This *is* a genius plan!" Josh declared.

CHAPTER 14

MORE THAN TWO OF EVERY ANIMAL

Out in the heather, Duncan showed Kit how to do some spells to round up animals. But it wasn't as easy as he made it look. Kit's magic wasn't misfiring or anything—she wasn't feeling any of that intense buildup of energy, and there were no laser blasts coming out of her eyes. She just . . . couldn't get the animals to follow her.

"You have to be gentle, Kit," said Duncan. "With this type of magic, it's not about control, it's about love. You have to show the animals kindness. You have to help them come with you."

"I don't think I have a gentle mode," said Kit.

"Try," said Duncan.

Kit grumbled and tried again, speaking the spell Duncan had showed her. She bowed down toward the creatures, opening out her arms and saying the spell word, *"Com!"*

She waited.

"Be gentle," said Duncan.

"OK, animals. I love you all. Now, come here! *Com!*"

Meanwhile, Alita had already found a colony of beetles and a pheasant, managing to tempt it onto her shoulder with some cookie crumbs. Dogon fluttered around making persuasive noises, too. Kit wasn't sure whether he was helping or getting in the way, but Alita was doing impressive work.

Kit only managed to persuade two rabbits and a worm to come with her in the end. And with the worm, it was less about persuasion and more about picking it up and carrying it.

Duncan kept the creatures with them, weaving his spells around them with murmured words. He drew a herd of deer toward them. The majestic creatures walked slowly over the purple heather, eyes bright and eager, making a strange low noise in their throats that sounded like something from the beginning of time.

"They're lovely!" said Alita.

One of the deer, a large stag with many-branched antlers, came over to her and bent his head. Alita nervously petted his neck. He made a snuffling sound.

"I think he likes you," said Duncan. He was giving Alita a strange look. "You really do seem to have a knack for this."

Alita giggled as the stag nuzzled her hand.

"This is literally her idea of heaven," said Kit.

"Well. Heaven can wait," said Duncan. "We have work to do."

They met Josh and Faith down by the lake just before four o'clock. Josh's jaw dropped as they approached. Even Faith looked deeply impressed.

"Well, Noah, you've got more than two of every animal there," she said to Duncan.

"I only got about two in total," said Kit. "Alita got tons!"

"Did she? Well done, Alita!" said Faith. She gave Alita an odd look, then glanced over to Duncan, who raised an eyebrow.

Alita looked puzzled. "What was that about?" she whispered to Kit.

"Dunno," said Kit. "Grown-ups always like having their secret languages."

A crowd of animals walked behind them. There were pheasants and deer, rabbits and grouse, as well as seabirds, summoned from the sea, and eagles and ospreys. Bees buzzed and butterflies flapped their multicolored wings. The ground crawled with insects, from beetles and ants to weevils and snails. (The snails brought up the rear.) Field mice and voles scuttled around them, and Highland cattle, Shetland ponies, and sheep tramped behind.

Duncan called a halt to his army of beasts with a gesture and a word. Dogon landed at the front of the army, puffing out his chest.

"Now," said Faith, "the bone." She made a

scooping gesture with her hand, and the bone rose up in its glowing magical case.

"Should we begin? Josh found the curse-breaking spell," said Faith. "It needs three wizards." Faith looked at Kit, her dark eyes shining. "What do you say, Kit?"

"But . . . I'm not safe," said Kit. "We still don't know what's making my magic flare up. Shouldn't Josh do it? If it's a written spell, he can do it, can't he?"

Josh shook his head. "Not this one. The book says it specifically needs wizards. Or the non-wizard person reading it explodes. And I don't want to explode."

"But what if my *magic* explodes and I hurt you all?" asked Kit.

"I believe in you," said Faith. "All you need to do is say the spell . . . and use as little of your power as you can. Almost try *not* to do magic. Just let the magic of nature do the work. Does that make sense?"

"I . . . think so," said Kit. Her heart was beating fast, like a speaker thumping a bass line in her chest.

"Let's begin," called Duncan. "The animals are

starting to get restless." Just then a pheasant squawked loudly, and a deer let out a throaty bellow.

The surface of the lake beyond them began to ripple, and the mermaids rose up.

"What's all that noise?" shrieked Morag. "Didn't we tell you to leave? Come closer and I'll bite you. We'll scratch out your eyes. LEAVE US, MORTALS!"

Faith ignored them as they kept yelling threats and promises of bites. "Take my hand," she said to Duncan.

Duncan took the hand she offered and nodded, showing that he was ready.

He beckoned the animals closer. Alita helped to herd them in the right direction, whispering to them.

Kit glanced at Faith. Faith nodded and reached out her hand to Kit. Kit took it as Faith whispered, "Don't be afraid. You have the power. You are safe. You can do this."

Kit wasn't sure. Was she making a horrible mistake?

Tingling power ran through her. Not Faith's

power. Her own power. She could feel it trying to burst out from her. But she pushed it down, thinking of her friends, of keeping them safe. *Just say the words*, she told herself. *Try not to do magic.*

They began to speak the spell.

A hum filled the air. The animals behind them shifted and rumbled. Alita stood beside them and stroked the face of the stag, whispering calming words.

Kit said the spell along with Duncan and Faith. She gripped their hands, as though holding on to a cliff edge with her fingertips. She pushed the magic inside her down and down to stop it from bubbling up.

Still, Kit felt that dreadful power rising. The more she spoke, the stronger the feeling became.

She heard a voice. It was coming from the bone. *"The child can't defeat us. She's holding back."* Kit heard echoing, high-pitched laughter.

The magic grew within her. The soft magic of nature flowed through the animals, through the earth, through the plants, through the air itself.

Was she holding back? Would the words be enough, if she squashed down her magic?

That voice was laughing again.

"We will win. We are winning! This spell has failed!"

I can't let them win! she thought. Kit let a little of the magic rise in her. She felt it building, until her whole body felt as though it were on fire.

"Kit, what's wrong?" Josh's voice sounded very far away.

From among the animals came the pitter-pattering of dozens of little feet. No, hundreds. Kit saw rats running from the army of animals toward the loch.

So. Many. Rats.

"She's losing control!" said Faith. She, too, sounded very far away. Everything in Kit was going into the spell. She couldn't let that voice defeat her. She wouldn't let the Dragon Masters win.

"Kit. Control your power," said Faith. "Don't let it burst out. Control your power. It's your power, not theirs."

"Let go," said the voice. *"Let it all go. Or you won't defeat us."*

Duncan and Faith began to speak the spell again. Kit joined in. She felt wave after wave of magic wash through her.

"The rats!" someone cried. "They're . . . joining."

Kit looked at the loch. On the water, the rats were climbing and clambering over one another. Floating on the water. Forming into another creature, made out of hundreds of rats.

A giant monster, seething, rising. A rat the size of a bear. Kit wanted to scream.

"So close," said the voice. *"Unleash your power. Free us."*

Kit felt as though the magic in her were about to explode. It would be so easy to just let go. To do what the voice wanted. "I don't think I can do this," she whispered.

Just then, she felt a tap on her shoulder. She paused and turned. Alita was there, with Dogon. She placed Dogon on Kit's shoulder and whispered, "Think of Dogon. Do this for all of us. Don't give up. Don't let go."

Someone gave her

arm a squeeze. Josh was standing there. "You've got this, Kit," he said.

The rat beast swayed across the water toward them.

"*Give up,*" said the voice. The voice of the rats, speaking as one. "*Give us our true shape. Release all your power into us. Bring us back to life. We are so close . . .*"

NO, thought Kit. *My friends believe in me. I believe in me. So I refuse to be bossed around by ghost rat wizards from the dawn of time. I'm Kit Spencer, and I am not afraid of you.*

In that moment, she realized something. Several somethings.

They lured me here, to Scotland. The Dragon Masters lured me here. They made the mermaids chase Lizzie away, knowing it would mess with my magic, knowing I'd follow the trail here. They need me here to bring them back. They've been taunting me, to get me to do what they want. They let me overhear them talking to the mermaids, about me being the only person who can beat them.

Well. They're right about that.

"ENOUGH!" she yelled.

"Kit?" whispered Faith, her face full of worry and pain. "Kit?"

"I'm OK," said Kit. "Let's finish this."

Faith nodded.

With that, Kit closed her eyes, pressed the rising magic down into the pit of her stomach, and spoke the last words of the spell in time with Duncan and Faith.

"BREAK!"

The mermaids shrieked with rage. A rage that sounded like it was from another world, another time. An ancient rage.

Another voice shrieked even louder. The voice of the Dragon Masters. The ghost wizards. The cursers of the bone. The controllers of the mermaids.

A shock wave whooshed across the loch. The rats scattered, falling apart and splashing into the water, swimming away, each alone. The scream of the Dragon Masters cut through the air and then, suddenly, fell silent.

The mermaids let out a very different cry. A whoop, almost. The glassy look in their eyes departed, and they surged forward, swimming joyfully.

"FREEEEEEE!" shrieked Morag. "We're FREE!"

"Freeeeee!" echoed the other merfolk.

The sky grew lighter. Sun broke through the clouds.

Kit saw dozens of rats swimming in different directions across the loch, making for dry land. There was no longer a single mind controlling them. They just wanted to get to safety.

"You *did* it!" said Faith.

"It worked!" cried Kit. "I didn't lose control!" She threw her arms around Faith in a hug of joy. Alita hugged them both, too, and Josh.

Duncan gestured to the animals. "Thank you!" he called.

With a whinny and a snuffle and a squawk and a peal of squeaks, they scattered, back to their lives.

"Is it over?" asked Josh.

"I think so," said Kit. "I think it is."

"What happened back there?" Faith asked Kit. "The rats . . . What were they?"

"I think . . . I think that was the Dragon Masters," said Kit. "They were trying to use my power to come back from the dead. They wanted me to lose control of my wild magic. I think that's what would have set them free."

"That must have been why they left the curse," said Josh, "as sort of an escape hatch, when they died. A way for them to come back one day, when someone disturbed their bones."

"I hope they didn't leave too many other cursed bones around," said Kit.

"Oh, you can bet that they did," said Faith grimly. "But we're safe for now."

"Uh . . . I'm not a hundred percent sure about that," said Alita. She pointed back at the lake.

Dark clouds were forming above the lake. Thunder rumbled in the distance. Then a huge fork of lightning slashed down, sizzling into the lake. Smoke rose from the surface of the water. Thick, swirling green smoke. Shapes formed in it. Kit thought that the shapes looked a little like skulls. The smoke writhed in and out of focus.

"What *is* that?" yelled Alita above the din of the thunder.

"WE ARE HERE," said a voice. Kit thought she saw a shape in the mist. A rat-like face. Another. A claw. A hint of a swishing tail.

"YOU BROKE OUR CURSE, BUT YOU CANNOT STOP US. WE WILL RETURN. WE WERE ALWAYS HERE. WE WILL FIND A WAY."

"Go AWAY!" yelled Kit. "You lost! I defeated you! Stop hanging around like a bad smell, you bunch of stinky evil ghost rats!"

There was a high-pitched, terrifying scream, and the clouds opened, rain hammering down on them. The faces in the smoke rushed toward Kit and through her, throwing her to the ground. She felt a chill rush through her, a horrible, horrible cold; she smelled fire and decay. She let out a cry, then felt hands pulling her to her feet. She looked back over her shoulder. The faces were gone. The mermaids had ducked beneath the water. There was nothing but the rain.

CHAPTER 15

CHOCOLATE TEA

Fifteen minutes later, they were sitting in Duncan's living room drinking some more chocolate tea. Duncan and Faith had done a drying spell on them, but they all still felt in need of warmth and comfort, and not just because the Scottish weather was on the cool side.

"Are you OK?" Josh asked Kit.

Kit shivered, remembering how it had felt when the rats had passed through her. "It felt . . . I can't put it into words," said Kit.

"Perhaps it's best not to," said Faith. "Words are powerful." She gave Kit a pat on the shoulder and got up, then strode over to where the bone lay in its carrying case.

She reached in and plucked the bone out.

Seeing the look of horror on the children's faces, she added, "It's perfectly safe now. We broke the curse. But, Duncan, you said this looks like a mammal's bone? A rat?"

Duncan's eyes went wide. "Of course. It's much too big to be a modern rat, but . . . a giant rat? Now we're talking."

"So the Dragon Masters were evil giant rats from the dawn of time?" asked Josh.

"Cool!" said Kit. Then, remembering the rats again, she shuddered.

Faith gave her an intent look. "You're safe now. And, I suspect . . ." She pulled something out of her pocket. It was her thaumometer. She pointed it at Kit, who flinched a little, afraid of what it might say.

The thaumometer glowed ever so slightly. Faith's face broke into a gigantic smile. "You're back to normal! I thought so!" she said.

"Really?" asked Kit. She felt a wash of relief,

followed by a little doubt. "Why is it still glowing, then?"

"Oh, your wild magic levels are always a little higher than the average wizard," said Faith, pocketing the thaum again. "You're a wild one, Kit Spencer. I think that's why the Dragon Masters chose you."

"They . . . chose me?" asked Kit. "Chose me for what?"

"They needed someone to release them back into this world," said Faith. "Someone with a naturally high store of wild magic. They wanted to ride back from the dead on a wave of your power."

"So that's why they were egging me on to let go during the spell?" Kit said. "I knew it!"

"Yes," said Faith. "They wanted you to let go! They scurried into your mind and threw your power out of balance. I wonder how, though?"

"My dream!" gasped Kit. "They came in through my dream! When I fell asleep at the table and dreamed of rats."

"Well, that's creepy," said Josh.

"Should we be worried that they said they'd be back?" asked Alita. "Will they try to get into Kit's dreams again?"

"They don't have an anchor in the world anymore," said Faith, "now that we've broken the curse that linked them to the bone. But if they try to get back another way, we'll be ready for them."

"I can't believe they *told* us they were coming back," said Josh. He made a disapproving clicking sound with his tongue. "Man, ancient evil giant rat ghosts need to watch more movies. Evil villains should never reveal their plans. It's what gets them caught in the end!"

"Well, there probably weren't many movies in ancient times," Alita pointed out, "so there's no way they could know that."

Kit couldn't help laughing. Although there was a shadow hanging over her, her friends were so silly that she couldn't feel too dark.

Faith put a hand on her shoulder and gave her a squeeze. "Well done, Kit. You beat them. You can go home soon. There's just one more thing to do."

Duncan drove them all back to the lochside, and they piled out of the van, Dogon on Alita's shoulder.

Faith nodded to Josh, and he began to sing. This time, it was a hymn. Something about ancient feet. Kit didn't know it.

As he sang, the lake rippled. The lochfolk rose slowly and cautiously out of the water.

"Yes?" said Morag. Her pale eyes peered out from between the curtains of her long weed-hair. She looked bleary, as though she'd only just woken up from a long, restless sleep. "What is it?" she snapped.

"We've come to ask if Lizzie can come home again," called Alita.

"And whether you mind going to fetch her," added Josh.

"Because I have to be home for dinner by six."

"Me too!" said Alita. "My ma is making fresh pakoras, so she's probably texted me about them, which is her way of saying 'don't be late' without actually saying it."

"And my mom will make me eat my dinner cold if I'm late," said Josh. "She learned that in a parenting book," he added, making a face. "The one type of book I *don't* like."

Morag looked at them blankly. "What's that? I'm feeling a bit funny. Could you repeat that?"

"I need to go home for dinner," repeated Josh. "Because my mom—"

"No, fool child, I mean, the part about Lizzie coming home. Is Lizzie not here? Where did she go?"

"You threw her out," said Kit.

"Don't you remember?" asked Alita. "You told her she wasn't welcome anymore, and you chased her away."

From the look on her face, Morag clearly did not remember. She looked at the humans like they were pulling her tail. "No, she was just here a minute ago . . ." Morag gave a nod to one of the other merfolk, and he dived down below the surface. A moment later he popped up again and gave Morag a shrug.

"Not here, ma'am!" he said.

Morag narrowed her eyes. "What's going on? I was just . . ." She trailed off. "I'm not sure what just happened. But it happened when a troop of meddling wizards turned up at my lochside, so it's probably your fault."

"No. It's really not," said Faith. "But . . . you don't remember anything?"

"Last thing I remember was finding a wee bone at the bottom of the loch. Didn't like the look of it. Threw it out." She gestured beyond the water. "Then . . ." She waved her webbed hands. "Nothing."

"You were under a curse," said Duncan. "We broke the curse."

Morag stared at him. "You what?"

"You were under a curse. We broke it. Now you can get Lizzie back and get your magic back," said Duncan. "A thank-you might be nice?" he suggested.

"HA!" trilled Morag. "Not likely. Where did Lizzie go?"

"You chased her away through a water portal," said Faith. "You should tell her to come back."

"Hmph! I suppose we will," said Morag. "Not because you asked, mind. Only because we want our magic back, so we can stop landscuttlers from coming and gawking at us like this," she said to the other merfolk. "Let's go and tell that pesky plesiosaur to come home."

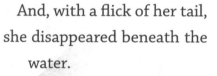

And, with a flick of her tail, she disappeared beneath the water.

"I thought that breaking the curse would stop them from being so mean," said Josh, looking disappointed.

A moment later, another head broke the surface of the lake. It was

Lizzie. She was grinning. "I don't know how you did it, but thank you!" said Lizzie. "Home sweet home!" She flapped her flippers and waggled her tail. "I was starting to feel really cramped in that little pond," she said. "So . . . thank you. I hope I didn't make too much of a mess. By the time I left . . . uh . . . some things were happening."

"Things?" asked Faith. She narrowed her eyes. "THINGS?"

"Yes. And stuff. BYE!" said Lizzie, swimming around and then diving quickly under the water, leaving a streak of ripples on the surface.

CHAPTER 16

HOME

They said goodbye to Duncan by the loch. He gave them each a paper bag full of homemade cookies before they left. When he came to Alita he said, "That was good work with the animals. You're a natural."

"I was thinking of being a magical vet when I grow up," said Alita, smiling shyly. "If I don't decide to be a dragon tamer. And if my parents don't mind."

"I'm sure we can find a way to persuade them," said Duncan, scratching behind Dogon's ears. Dogon gave a chirruping sound and pushed against

Duncan's hand, encouraging more scratches.

"He'll make you do that all day if you don't watch out." Faith laughed. "Come on, Dogon. Get in the van. Time to go home." She patted the side of the mobile library.

"I'll get the portal book!" said Kit, excitedly browsing the shelves to find the computer book they'd used to get here.

"Kit, excited about books," said Josh, shaking his head. "It's a funny world."

Back at their own library, they decided to check up on the "mess" Lizzie claimed to have left behind before they all went home. When they reached the park gate, the scene that met them was out of control. The park was crawling with talking animals. Not just talking—some of them were singing. A flock of pigeons was singing a rude version of the national anthem. Fish from the lake were riding on the backs of turtles. A troop of ants had formed a marching band.

And worse, ordinary people were noticing it.

Sunburned people were wandering around in a daze, pointing at animals and blinking.

"I think I have sunstroke," said one woman.

"Should have drunk more water at that picnic," a man was saying.

"We need to shut this down *now*," hissed Faith. "A magic-calming spell for starters. Kit, repeat it after me, and go the other way around the park. Each time you cast it, it should affect every animal within earshot."

"*Ruo onwe gi,*" said Faith.

When Faith finished, the pigeons stopped singing and went back to chirping. The fish flopped back into the lake. The ants on the ground stopped chattering.

Kit listened carefully, then copied Faith, repeating the spell and doing the gestures—with Alita and Josh in tow, correcting her pronunciation when she got it wrong.

As they passed and Kit cast her spell, the animals went back to normal. Any people they passed looked dazed, shaking their heads.

When they'd gone all around one half of the park, they met up with Faith again, who'd finished her half and was sitting on a bench by the gate. "All done?" she asked.

Kit nodded. "What about the people? Were you putting a forgetting spell on them?"

"No need," said Faith. "In hot weather like this, people will convince themselves it was all in their heads. If this had been winter, when people are sharper, we would've been in trouble. So say thanks to the sunshine!" She gestured to the sky, turning up her face to the lowering sun.

Just then a dog trotted past, following a larger dog, and said, "I smell a nice butt!"

Kit blushed. "Uh . . . I think I missed that one."

"It's OK. I've got it," said Faith. She said the spell one last time, and the dog stopped talking and started barking.

"So," said Kit. "We defeated the ghost rats from the dawn of time. We saved the mermaids from a curse, sent Lizzie home, and helped Dogon, too. What do we do next? How do we get ready in case they come back?"

"We do what we've *been* doing," said Faith. "We learn. We train."

"And we read?" asked Josh.

"And we read." Faith laughed.

"Yay!" said Alita.

"Whatever else changes, whatever threats we face," said Faith, "we will always have books."

Kit was surprised to find that she found that very comforting indeed.

✳ WHICH CHARACTER FROM ✳ THE MONSTER IN THE LAKE ARE YOU?

Now that you've read the book,
it's time to take the quiz.

1. What's your favorite food or drink?

    A. Whatever's closest to where I'm reading!

    B. Food that's not cruel to animals

    C. All of it!

    D. Chocolate tea

    E. Fresh-baked bread

    F. We feast on the whimpering cries of humanity.

2. What's your favorite type of book?

    A. Anything in the Danny Fandango series

    B. Anything in the Danny Fandango series

    C. Short ones with pictures

    D. That's for me to know and you to find out.

    E. A recipe book!

    F. The book of YOUR DOOM

3. What is the meaning of life?

   A. Reading!

   B. Helping animals. Oh, and people.

   C. Having adventures and climbing trees

   D. What do YOU think it is?

   E. Protecting our planet

   F. Ruling your planet

4. What are your thoughts on mermaids?

   A. They are fascinating! I've read so many AMAZING books on them.

   B. Some people call them monsters but actually there's no such thing as a monster. That's just a word humans use for creatures they don't like.

   C. They're not all glamorous like in books. They're SCALY and RUDE. So that's cool.

   D. It's best to treat them with intense politeness.

   E. Grumpy lads and lasses, best avoided

   F. Foolish, petty creatures that are easy to manipulate into doing your bidding

✳ **If you answered mostly As:**

> You are **JOSH**.
>
> You love books more than almost anything else.

✳ **If you answered mostly Bs:**

> You are **ALITA**.
>
> You love animals more than most people and you're caring and passionate.

✳ **If you answered mostly Cs:**

> You are **KIT**.
>
> You're enthusiastic and always mean well, even when you mess up.

✳ **If you answered mostly Ds:**

> You are **FAITH**.
>
> You are smart, powerful, and occasionally mysterious, with a dry sense of humor and expressive eyebrows.

✳ **If you answered mostly Es:**

    You are **DUNCAN.**

    You are kindly, environmentally conscious, and love to cook.

✳ **If you answered mostly Fs:**

    You are a **DRAGON MASTER.**

    You are an evil ghost rat from the dawn of time and I hope you're ashamed of yourself, you fiend!

✳ ACKNOWLEDGMENTS ✳

The idea of a solitary genius writer is nonsense—every book is a team effort. This is my team.

Thanks to Polly, my agent, for all the support and encouragement. Thank you to Davide, my cocreator, who adds layers to my characters that I hadn't even imagined, from lumberjack shirts to 8-bit style scenes. Thank you to Tom, my editor, for preventing my characters from exploding like Mr. Creosote due to an improbable number of meals, even though it pained him to take away cake from a story.

Thank you to Elisabetta, my designer, and to the whole Nosy Crow team who make, sell, promote, market, and generally push my books into the world. Rebecca, special thanks to you for something that's not technically about this book—but for all your help getting book one out there. I'm sorry I didn't bring you back any gingerbread from Grasmere.

Thank you to my early readers, Ammara and Samantha, for shaping the world of the library with me.

Thank you to the Girls, as always, and the puppies, who know all the secrets and must keep our pact of mutually assured destruction. Thank you to Team Swag for all the cheerleading and for Cowell Finn. Thank you to Aisha and the rest of the gang for an outlet. Thank you to the pocket friends for higs. And thank you to the entire internet, especially those 30–50 feral hogs, for distracting me when writing was too hard, until I was ready to face it again.

ABOUT THE AUTHOR & ILLUSTRATOR

LOUIE STOWELL started her career writing carefully researched books about space, ancient Egypt, politics, and science, but eventually she lapsed into just making stuff up. She likes writing about dragons, wizards, vampires, fairies, monsters, and parallel worlds. Louie Stowell lives in London with her wife, Karen; her dog, Buffy; and a creepy puppet that is probably cursed.

DAVIDE ORTU is an Italian artist who began his career in graphic design before discovering children's book illustration. He is on a quest to conjure colorful and fantastic places where time stops to offer the biggest emotions to the smallest people. Davide Ortu lives in Spain.